DUST TO DUST

A SHORT NOVEL
BY M.C. NORRIS

READ UNTIL YOU BLEED!

DEDICATION

Dad,

Think of this book as a bumper crop of memories harvested from the mind of the man whose influence shaped both our lives and our characters; memories in regard to his personal experiences during the Dust Bowl era, as a wheat farmer in the heart of Kansas. We're talking about Grandpa, of course.

It took about a year's worth of visits with one of the best men you and I were ever privileged to know, during what would turn out to be his last good year of life out there on the same farm where you grew up, and where that guy always belonged. In the end, I collected what I needed to create what I hope to be an authentic setting, one loaded with Easter eggs for those lucky enough to have known your dad, and one corrupted with an infusion of vampire horror, which—had Grandpa lived to have read this book, would have just confused the holy Hell out of him, and that rather amuses me.

This one is for you, Dad, in fond memory of him.

- Love, Michael

PART ONE OF SIX:

SIX INCHES TO HELL

"The town of Eden's just a fig leaf that barely covers the ugly truth," the minister said. He glowered down over a modest congregation of farmers and their families, and he sucked the grit from his teeth. Thick fingers gripped the pulpit until his knuckles turned white as hailstones. "Just step outside, and have a look around you. Take a good look at those fields of dust and ash. The good Lord never meant for those plains to meet your till. Grasslands were made for grazing. That's how's come all them buffalo were here. The best side was already up, brothers and sisters, and you turned it all upside-down." He lurched over his candlelit pages, narrowing his eyes at his parishioners. "We slaughtered the last buffalo, run off the Indians, and plowed up every inch of topsoil. For all that trouble, what do we got?" he asked.

His features softened in the flickering light. "Hell, brothers and sisters. Check the depth of your plow, because we're just six inches from Hell."

Just like that, them browned sheets tacked over the church windows got to flapping like sailcloth in a squall. A dusky pall settled in that blanched the color of things. The boy could feel something gathering in the air, just as plain as the filth that coated his tongue. Weird energy fished from one body to the next, crackling right up through folks' hair. Made him want to sidle close to Pap and cling hard to his leg, but he knew better than to touch another while a black duster was rolling over, or you were liable to get a jolt so bad as to knock you both to the ground.

Rumbling swelled in the west 'til a map of veins bulged from the minister's forehead in his effort to shout over the roar. The temperature was dropping fast. The air soon felt so cold that it wouldn't have surprised a soul if Lucifer himself appeared right there in their midst. Fear slackened faces and upturned eyes, as fairy lights began to flicker overhead like tongues of Pentecostal fire.

The corner of a tacked bed sheet tore loose from beyond the pulpit. In an instant, the storm ripped the whole mess free, converting sheet and shutters to the wind's wild religion, and transforming the window into some godforsaken portal blown agog on its hinges. Outside, the play of lightning was both awesome and terrifying to behold, as a wall of electric filth trundled over them, spinning like a twister on its side. Tons of topsoil sucked off the tops of their sorry fields was spewed half-a-mile into the sky. It appeared to mock them, as it left their farms behind to join the thunderous amalgam of earth, wind and fire.

One by one, the minister's candles flickered out. The pages of his bible began to flip with a life all their own, as if that unseen devil in their midst meant to skim clean through all the good and decent parts straight to the Book of Revelation. Outside, Pap's favorite mule began to bray.

Pap nudged the boy. "Come on. Gotta go check on Simon's tether."

The boy dogged his Pap's heels down the center aisle. When his old man threw open that church-house door, what a vision awaited him on the other side. Backlit by hot wires of electricity, a masked and goggled Enis Goddard and his haggard knot of hands stood poised and leering into that sanctuary of churchgoers like gang of damned gunslingers belched straight up from Hell.

The boy stole a peek at the face of God, as folks called old Enis, when he dropped his bandana to flash his gold-toothed grin. God gave a little chuckle as Pap pardoned past. He poked his fingers down into the front pouch of his overalls, and he withdrew a folded square of newspaper. He offered it furtively to the boy, as if the thing in his hand might be a ticket to some strange show. The boy noticed his own affrighted reflection gawping back from the greenish lenses of God's aviator goggles.

"Read this," God said, "and then, you'd best go and tell your Pap that he's running out of time to do the right thing."

As the boy reached out, a hot bridge of static spat between his and God's fingertips, merging their energies in an instant. A terrible brilliance whitewashed Main Street and beyond, as a thunderclap hit so hard that it shook the church to its limestone footings. The heavens dropped to earth in a fiery pillar that fused sand to glass, man-flesh to beast, as Pap's scream accompanied that of his mule in an awful chord of anguished dissonance.

⸻

Sometimes the right course of action runs clear as pumped water, clear as the stars that had shined so brightly the following eve that a boy could read newsprint by starlight alone. Such terrible clarity, not a day after the worst duster of all time had rolled over the state of Kansas like a combine's header. It was a day that would forever be remembered as Black Sunday.

By the stars, what a newspaper article it was. Enis Goddard never let on as to why he'd thought to give a boy such an awful thing, but by dawn's break, it seemed pretty obvious there was more to some folks than met the eye. What to do with the information had never been the question. It was when and how, and those were the sorts of questions that lingered worst in the night's darkest hours, when the centipedes got to scratching inside the walls. God's gift had planted a seed in the boy's mind, but it didn't offer much advice on how to propagate it. Felt just as desperate as trying to raise a decent crop of wheat during the worst drought that had ever come to pass. It was the sort of work that had to be done, but there sure wasn't an easy way to go about it.

The boy snapped out of his daydream. He was almost glad for an excuse to quit the field when the big day he'd been so worried about finally arrived, because there was God's Model A pickup purring straight toward the crossroads. The boy looked to the sullen skies for the time of day, but there was no sun. He yanked a spear of pigweed, and he chunked it much further than it ought to have travelled with a little help from the wind. Smearing his palms against his trousers, he loped through the thin rows of wheat toward the road.

Yella Dog rose from her wallow and shook herself off in a dust-billowing, ear-flapping shimmy. A jackrabbit flushed at the commotion. It kicked its blanched heels forty yards before freezing and glancing back, statuesque, like the cover of a children's book. The wind bullied its ears and fur, but it didn't move. Nothing stared quite like a jackrabbit. Yella Dog fawned mindlessly up at the boy, licking at his knuckles, and looking just as dumb as a sack of hammers.

"Go on and get him, you knucklehead. Rabbit, sitting right there."

As the boy glowered out over the scorched field, he recalled Pap once saying that if your wheat didn't hide a jackrabbit by Easter, then it wasn't going to be worth a shit, come harvest. Here it was, already June. But a good yield hardly mattered when the price per bushel was down to almost twenty cents, below the cost to propagate it. Wouldn't even make it into the grain elevator. Half the country was starving. Food riots were popping off down in Oklahoma and Arkansas while whole mountains of last season's wheat sat rotting at every train station. Didn't make any sense. Something was off, a few rungs up the ladder.

The boy narrowed a mean eye at the rabbit. He pantomimed a baseball bat slicing through its spindly neck. He clicked his tongue at the point that his fantasy bat would've struck the varmint, and then he exhaled the imagined crowd's roar as its lop-eared head sailed out over left field, over the fence, and gone.

God's automobile drew closer. The sound of the Model A's engine seemed to lag by a quarter-mile, like a phantom growling emanating from his trail of dust. Beyond the crossroads, electricity pulsed at the heart of a black wall that was starting to loom in the west. Looked like it was going to be another bad one. This would make for the nineteenth duster in as many days. The town was all but shut down. Fields were empty. Folks had given up and gone. No one in all the world but he and God, it appeared, were foolish enough to be out and about on a day of reckoning like this.

Although the boy had caught glimpses of him, he hadn't spoken a word to God since Black Sunday. Just as well. Their willful avoidance of one another had afforded the boy some time to mull things over in his head, to carefully choose the words he was going to say to God, and to prepare for whatever might follow.

The boy shielded his eyes from the blowing grit and gazed out across Pap's miserable section. The tidal wave of filth had just begun to roll. Wouldn't be long, now. The boy scowled at the last of God's telephone poles, standing there at the edge of their property line like a border guard. It was the only man-made obstacle for who knows how many square miles, so it was hard to avoid looking at that constant reminder of the man he hated to think about. As he strode past the pole, the boy's arm rose to push off of it, but his palm stopped just short of touching the thing. He froze, awing over the pole's rippling dragon hide with an equal measure of fascination and revulsion.

There were millions of them. All clustered on the shady north side of the pole as one scabrous layer, they appraised the blasted landscape through their blood blister

8

eyes. The boy could hear their chirring mouthparts nipping at the wood. The boy reached into his boot. He withdrew the Comanche arrow that he always kept holstered there. He leveled its stone tip directly at the hoppers, as if it weren't an old arrow at all, but a powerful wizard's wand. Where his shadow fell upon the pole, the column shifted, jostling to occupy the new shaft of darkness. Articulating legs sidestepped with the mechanical synchrony of an army of tiny robots. The boy lowered his wand, and stuffed it back down inside of his boot. It was an afternoon of quiet portents.

God's Model A turned at the crossroads, and began purring his way. The boy glanced at the approaching pickup, then back at the pole. He lashed out with a flat-footed kick, crushing a dozen beneath his boot. Their snotty guts smeared the wood. He wrinkled his nose with a sort of satisfied revulsion, and kicked again, killing less this time. A million hoppers flung themselves into the gritty wind, splay-legged and crackling. Where they'd all been chewing, the pole looked polished and new. Thunder resonated deep and mean through the earth and cooling air.

The boy goose-stepped through the bordering pig-weeds in the direction of the brush pile. Yella Dog anti-cipated their destination, and went snuffling ahead. There was a water jug stashed on the north side of it that he hoped might still be a little cool. God's pickup was about to beat him there. The boy ran, as if it were a race to the drink. A whole bunch of God's filthy hands were all piled in back of the truck. Every one of them looked to be carrying a bat, a chain, or some kind of a damned whopping stick. The pickup rolled to a stop beside the boy. Dim and grinning minions leered down from their perch on the truck's sidewalls. The boy saw his reflection doubled in God's aviator goggles.

"There's going to be a drive this afternoon, if you'd like to come along," God said, flashing his gilded grin.

He looked across the pickup's cab at the man in the passenger seat. His sunken chest rose and fell, as he cupped an unsteady hand over a dusty jar of hooch, and licked the mud from the corners of his mouth. His eyes were dulled by fermented corn to a state of sinful complacence.

"Don't you reckon they might call it, on account of the storm?" the boy inquired. He knew that Pap would've skinned him alive for even considering going for a ride with this wild bunch, who never quit work or play on account of a duster. He guessed they'd probably set fifty telephone poles over the last nineteen days, until the line came to a halt at the edge of Pap's section. Why they picked up such a crazy pace during the worst bouts of weather was beyond him. It was almost as if God's crewmen were motivated by the added difficulty that the dust storms contributed. Some men were just hard that way. The boy squinted and cocked his head at God, the richest man in four counties.

"Nope," God replied. "It's my drive, and there ain't nobody going to call nothing. How old a boy are you, anyhow?"

"Ten."

"Ten, you say?"

The boy nodded, sucking his teeth.

God scratched at his chin. "Then, I guess you probably ain't never even been to a rabbit drive, have you?"

"No, sir."

"Got anything to club a rabbit with?"

10

The boy spun and leapt into the ditch. He crashed through the mishmash, and then clambered up the opposite side. Crackling hoppers took to flight. He snatched up his tools, all wrapped in a yard of burlap to protect their handles from the gnawing bugs. He took up his water jug and almost dropped it when several red-eyed hoppers crawled right out through the open bung onto the back of his hand. The damned cork was gone. He'd forgotten to wrap the jug in burlap, and the little bastards had gnawed the whole cork away. The boy could remember a time, not so very distant, when Pap would've been awfully sore over a screw-up like this.

The boy knew where he could find a replacement, a rubber one that not even the grasshoppers could eat. Back in the old schoolhouse stores, buried amongst all that other junk, was a cedar chest filled with all sorts of interesting stuff, including a bunch of rubber stoppers. The trouble was that Pap had gotten so angry over the quiver of Comanche arrows he'd borrowed that the boy's stomach took a tumble at the thought of returning to that school-house again. Under Pap's scornful eye, he'd returned what little he'd taken, and apologized to the Historical Guild. However, he'd secretly kept the best arrow—just one— because it was the best thing he'd ever held in his hands.

"You coming along, or what?"

"Yes, sir," the boy said, shaking off the daydreams.

The memory of Pap's once fitful temperament got him smiling and staring into the weeds. A real firecracker he'd been. So much had changed since last season that it physically stilled him into a lull whenever he got to thinking about all that had once been. Seemed as if the better part of the world he'd always known had all just blown away with the topsoil, and scattered into the wind.

The boy hugged his water jug and tool bundle to his chest, as he crunched back through the weed-choked ditch, and back onto the road. There, he hesitated, when one of the men muttered something in Spanish. The boy crinkled his eyes at the brown faces clustered over the pickup's wooden sidewalls. Grime muted most expressions, but it heightened the effect of smiles. He lifted his gear up to them, and they took it.

"Say," God hollered, "come back on around here for just a minute, why don't ye."

The boy smeared his hands on the front of his overalls. He ducked his eyes, as he shuffled up to the driver's side window. This was it, he reckoned. Everything in these parts took its own sweet time, and everything had a certain formality, especially long overdue confrontations.

God removed the unlit cigar. He leaned out the window, and he spat with a strange precision into the dirt. "Out there at the drive," God said, "you watch out for those sons-of-bitches. You hear me?"

The boy cocked his head. He'd shot a mess of jack-rabbits and they hardly seemed a thing to fear. Maybe it was different when you had a thousand of them corralled and half-crazed, getting their brains bashed out against a wire fence.

"Some of them boys are liable to be drunk, and they'll all be swinging clubs."

"Oh, alright," the boy said, chewing the inside of his lip.

"Stick close, and you'll be just fine. Might even have a little fun."

"Yes, sir."

God peered down at Yella Dog. The vapid-eyed mutt looked to the boy, as if for some sort of instruction. "Gonna load your hound?"

"No, sir. She'd follow us clear to the North Pole, if you drove that far."

God snorted, and nodded his head. "How about you ride up front with the two of us? Maybe you'll get to steer a little."

The boy smiled, eyes brightening.

God popped the door and slid out onto the road, allowing access to the middle of the front seat. The boy had never ridden in a Ford before. He'd poked his head inside of one once, when a big shot down at the creamery had seen him staring, and had invited him over to come and have a look. At the time, the boy was too dirty to feel right about climbing into it, or touching anything. Today wasn't much different, but at least God was a local, so he understood.

As the boy settled into his seat, he couldn't quit smiling. It felt so funny to finally be sitting inside of an automobile. A few families around Eden had cars, and most farmers had a tractor, but not Pap. Pap remained partial to a mule-drawn cultivator. "Ain't no tractor ever built," Pap used to proclaim, when he was still able to talk, "that can match the heart of a good Missouri mule."

God hauled himself into the driver's seat and slammed the door, squashing the boy between the two men. The boy glanced furtively over at the man in the passenger seat. He recognized him as one of the drunkards from down at the train station. He smelled just as ripe as a sliced onion. The boy frowned at the canning jar between the man's thighs. The fellow noticed, and he offered it. The boy tried to appear casual as he accepted the jar, and hoisted the filthy vessel to his mouth.

Two summers ago, Pap bought a quart of White Lightning off a broom corn Texan he'd met up at the fair. As soon as Pap took the mules afield, the boy was quick to steal a sip of it. Good God almighty, that first drink should have cured any normal person outright of the desire to ever touch alcohol again. However, there was something alluring about grown men's vices, even after they proved terrible.

The boy winced as the fumes seared his wind-burned eyes, stiffening as liquid fire sluiced over the back of his tongue. When he pulled the jar away, exhaling hotly through his teeth, he noticed God grinning around that fat cigar, and he heard the whooping of all the field hands in back. They drummed their fists on the dusty side rails and stomped their feet, passing around jars of their own. The boy smiled. He pulled another swig. It was easier the second time. It felt like he'd just passed an initiation of sorts, and life had never felt so grand. Ruined wheat raced to the edge of infinity, and no one cared.

The boy felt an elbow nudge his ribs. He returned the jar of hooch back to its owner. Lightning danced through Train Station Man's jar, as the fellow drank. His rolling eyes tilted skyward. Only his plunging Adam's apple disrupted his peaceful countenance. His left hand lay up-turned and lifeless in his lap. Dark crescents of earth were impacted beneath his nails. Stitch-studded scars ran up the inside of his wrist like a railroad track.

"So, how goes it?" God asked.

The boy shrugged. "Same as ever."

The Model A purred through the wastelands between Pap's section and Eden, transporting them like busload of tourists on a sightseeing excursion through some lost and forsaken land. Today, the depravity was not theirs to own, and it felt darned good to be divorced from it. Their miserable lives seemed nothing more than strange scenery from the cab of a Model A. One field in wheat to another three in potatoes, left unturned and abandoned. Tumbleweeds hurtled across Black Bill's section, where his cultivator remained where he'd abandoned it, like some wayward vessel come to rest on the ocean floor. Not a single tree in all creation. Nothing but barbed wire to break the keening wind. The unstrung procession of God's telephone poles sprouted one after another from the horizon. Each seemed to grow tall, and slide by. Fat hawks surmounted them like buffed targets in a shooting gallery.

Pap used to joke about God's telephone poles, calling them "grasshopper roosts." God and his crew began setting those poles as far out as the original dugout settlements, as if he anticipated some new tenants would soon be occupying those ruins. Folks said God practically lived up the new phone office in Liberal, where it had taken some pretty dogged determination to win them over on stringing lines westward into the dead corner of Kansas.

Despite all his efforts, the brush pile at the edge of Pap's property was where God's project was halted. Twice, Pap refused God's offers for a strip of easement along the edge of his section. For Pap, it was a matter of pride over money. Balking God might be the first and last time in Pap's life that he could hope to exert some measure of control over a rich and powerful man. So, he did, and his property line was where God's procession of telephone poles petered out. Long as Pap had anything to say about it, that brush pile was as close to Liberal's telephone office as God was ever going to get.

Oh, but God was smug. He'd leased ten thousand acres at a premium just after the war, while the government was still guaranteeing prices at two dollars a bushel. Then, folks called him the devil incarnate when the wheat prices plunged straight to hell. Say what you will about God, but he was a survivor. He'd made a hard gamble, hunkered down out there in the old Comancheria, and called those wastelands home until he gained the upper-hand over all the latecomers. He was shrewd enough to be the devil, so maybe in fact he was. Odds were, his investment in telephone poles was going to pay off too, eventually.

"Seen you hung new tarpaper on your place," God said. "Looks nice."

"Had to," the boy said, treating himself to another big pull off the jar, "because we had the danged centipedes so bad this spring that taking a flat iron to the walls wouldn't cure them. Pouring kettles of boiling water around the outside wouldn't knock them back neither, but that big duster that come through last month, the one that brought us the baseball-sized hail?"

"Yeah?"

"Knocked so many danged holes in the tarpaper that I ain't had no choice but to replace it all." The boy shook his head. The liquor was starting to make him feel talkative, dizzy. "I was glad of it, too."

"How's come you was so glad?"

"Well shit, makes it hard for a guy to sleep with all them centipedes a-chewing all night long. Almost sounds like there's something bad out there, trying to get in."

"You're a brave young man."

The boy looked at God.

"You are."

Whatever feral energy fueled that manipulator of men seemed to burn just beyond those tinted lenses, and for a moment it set God's goggles aglow. The boy swallowed, and turned his head back to the road. While Train Station Man tipped back his murky potion, the boy's hand crept down to his hidden arrow. Sometimes, he just liked to touch it. It made him feel braver just to verify that his weapon was ready and waiting inside his boot. A blonde coyote loped across the road, and then melted into a grassy swale. The boy could still see it, looking back.

"Anyone helping you look after your Pap?"

"Cobbs do. J.P. farms our east eighty, and Martha comes around pretty regular, even cooks for us sometimes."

"Good neighbors?"

"The very best."

"How's your ol' Pap getting along, anyhow? Has he talked at all, yet?"

The boy shook his head. "Not much since the lightning strike. Doc says he might not walk or talk right ever again."

"Well, that's a damned shame." God adjusted his goggles. "You ever get a chance to read that newspaper article I passed off to you on Black Sunday, just before your ol' Pap got struck down?"

The boy frowned at God, and then pulled a swig off the jar. "Yes, sir. I did."

"What'd you think of it?"

The boy shrugged. "Guess I found it a little confusing."

God shifted his grip on the steering wheel, studied the boy for a spell, and then looked back to the dusty road. "How so?"

"Well, it talked about a mass grave they'd found, west of town, back in all them old ruins. Said they reckoned them bones might not be so old, after all. Said they might even belong to folks who we'd figured had moved back east, like ol' Black Bill. Like they'd all just been killed, or something."

God cleared his throat. "It's a strange thing, ain't it, when you realize things ain't what they seem? Frightening, even. That's exactly why I brought you along with me today." God reached over and tousled the boy's hair. Dust rained from his bangs down into the liquor jar. "I never could talk with your ol' Pap. He hated my guts and liver. Same could be said about Black Bill, and just about everyone else who ever lived along this goddamned stretch of road. They all hated me, and for what? Because I wanted to run a telephone line through Eden, introduce y'all to some new technology?"

"I don't know that anyone *hated* you, really ..."

"Boy, I'm no farmer, not like you and your Pap, anyhow, but in a bigger kind of way, we ain't so very different. I'm just a different sort of farmer, and I like to think of Eden as my crop. My fine crop of wheat. Just like in any field, you're going to get some hogweed, some mustard, and some tumbleweed. The old-timers used to pickle and eat tumbleweed. Can you imagine that? Folks think times is tough now, huh. Century ago, you'd huddle around a burning buffalo chip and eat pickled weeds all through the winter. Jackrabbits fared better. Those were the worst hard times, son. Not these. But even way back then, when there wasn't but a sod roof between what few of us were out here and the Comanche, folks still found reason to hate me." God rolled his cigar between his lips, then nipped off the end between his gold incisors and shrugged, chewing the plug thoughtfully before spitting the quid out the window. He beckoned to Train Station Man, who dipped into his overalls and fished out a box of matches. "Today, my big push is progression away from those hard times, and progress is something that you mule-drivers just don't seem to appreciate."

The boy glanced wide-eyed at God, and then back at the road again.

"That service contract I been waiting for, from the telephone office in Liberal? Well, turns out it's time to start stringing some lines. They're primed to contract the first builder who runs a line to their doorstep. Winds of change are a-blowing, son, and they're blowing hard up against your section." God hitched his eyebrows. Train Station Man popped a grimy thumbnail against the match head. "Y'all would've skinned out of Eden right after Black Sunday, I'd guess, if that bolt hadn't struck your Pap down. See, I meant to deliver your Pap a clear message, right there on the church house steps, when I had a few of my boys knock the brains out of that mule of yours."

"Simon ..."

God shook his head and clicked his tongue. "But then, down come a bolt of lightning. I wouldn't know what the odds are of that happening right when it did, but what I surely do know is that paralyzed men ain't no good for business. They can't be reasoned with, bought or threatened. Kind of left me in a queer spot. You know what I mean?"

"I know you been coming around our farm, Mr. Goddard." The boy spoke to the road, eyes straight ahead. "I know you been coming around, most every night since Black Sunday, and I ain't afraid of you."

Train Station Man popped his thumbnail and the match spat pink flame. He extended the burning stick across the boy's chest to meet with the end of God's cigar. Puffing his cheeks like a bellows, God filled the Model A with a brimstone stink.

"Son, it's about harvest time, and I've been in the business of farming *people* long enough that I know when it's time to get out there and yank a few fuckin' weeds." God lowered his goggles. He glared at the boy through a set of coyote-yellow eyes. "By now, I guess you've figured we ain't taking you to no rabbit drive."

The boy could sense that the hands in back were all listening, watching, and waiting for some sort of a signal. His heart got to chugging in his ears until his mouth ran dry. This was it.

Train Station Man leered, his gray tongue questing the corner of his mouth. As if suddenly graced with a mighty fine idea, the drunkard reached behind his back, and withdrew an enormous knife. Smiling, he turned it to and fro while the slab of curved steel borrowed fire from his flickering match. It glimmered like a January plow blade, honed and eager to till some ruts.

"Just look at this storm," God whispered, grinning in the cooling air as the wave of electrified earth loomed over them. "My lord, but it's going to be a beauty."

Train Station Man giggled. His hair was standing on end. Lightning gleamed in his moonshine eyes, and flashed along the edge of his blade. The hired hands in back began to whoop and holler as a tempest blacker than a cellar of canned midnight thundered upon them.

"Cut him," God growled, his yellow eyes burning from within their dark pits. He pulled a draw off his stogie until the cherry glowed hot and bright. "Cut his heart out. I want it pickled in a jar."

The boy lunged. He pitched the grain alcohol straight into the devil's face, blowing wide Hell's gates to reclaim him. Inhuman screams accompanied the roar of flames. Whatever the thing called "Enis Goddard" really was, it did not seem to be impervious to fire. The boy rolled right over the drunkard's lap, pinning his knifed hand to the seat as he popped the door, and barrel-rolled straight out into the ditch.

Weeds and gravel stripped hide from the boy's windmilling arms and legs. Finally stopped, spitting dirt, he raised his head to see those fellows in the truck bed backlit by the inferno within the cab. Train Station Man tumbled burning out the passenger door. His body folded strangely as the Model A rolled over him. The flaming pickup disappeared into the warring elements like a taxicab for the damned.

The boy flattened himself in the ditch, crawling in search of shelter. Plenty of folks died in these dusters. Their corpses sometimes turned up days later, with both lungs filled with mud. If the blowing filth didn't suffocate you outright, it could blind you, or kill you months later from dust pneumonia. God and his ship of fools were the only folks around without the sense to take cover when a duster loomed, and you never saw God with the same crew twice. God was always the last man standing. In fact, the only time you really ever saw the man afoot was on those days that a black duster had swallowed up all the daylight—that, or after sundown.

The boy hitched his overalls up over his nose and mouth, scrunched his eyes shut, and dragged himself forward. Stinging pellets of ice and windblown sand seared his skin, but he pressed forward, sweeping his arm along the road's shoulder until at last, he found what he'd been searching for. Clawing drifted dust from the pipe's end, he then forced his way into the drainage culvert, while retching up filth from his lungs. The corrugated cylinder was barely wider than his shoulders. It was so badly collapsed beneath the weight of the road that he could only inch forward with his head cocked to one side, but at least the air was breathable. He could even open his eyes.

He stared down the pipe to the culvert's opposite end, where he could see the spectral energy pulsing. Static snapped in the air. Tons of falling topsoil poured down, from above. The boy closed his eyes and tried to imagine a bluebird day, where gentle Kansas breezes harped through a prairie grass infinity, but the tonnage of falling filth resonated like the thundering hooves of a bygone buffalo herd, driven by spectral shrieks of Comanche wind. The wailing tempest was suddenly muffled. The boy's eyes flicked open. The culvert had darkened, as if a cork had just been stuffed into the leeward end. Something else was crawling in.

Claws raked against corrugated metal. The boy could smell its sour wildness, and could hear the mud bubbling in its lungs. Static tendrils spat up from its back to crackle against the culvert walls. The boy pushed away, reversing direction, but dust had already sealed him in from behind. He kicked against the slough of fine dust that had acquired the density of damp concrete. The thing was almost upon him. He hitched up his right knee and raked at the cuff of his overalls, groping wildly for the weapon that he'd kept stashed in his boot ever since Black Sunday, ever since his little epiphany beneath the stars, when he'd come to an uncertain conclusion as to what Enis Goddard might really be. The thin shaft rolled against his fingertips.

"Yella Dog?"

A thin whine came in response, followed by a great hack of mud. The dog smacked its chops, and then attempted to shake the dust from its fur as best as the cramped quarters would allow.

"Shit the bed, Yella Dog," the boy exclaimed, wrestling the mutt's shaggy head until it released a lapping tongue and hot chuffs of doggy breath. It was her, alright. "You scared the bejeezus out of me."

Hands, cold as hailstones, seized the boy's ankles in a grip so powerful that it halted the flow of blood to his feet. He felt the warm shag of Yella Dog pull loose from his embrace, as clawed manacles dragged him back through drifted dust, and out into the storm.

There it stood. Blasted by sand and blowing grit, the naked thing seething over him appeared to be quite at home, in Hell. One wolfish eye still burned in the blackness, while its neighbor had burst and boiled over, oozing like fried egg down its charred cheek. Its lips parted with a reptilian hiss. Sprays of electrical sparks flitted from the golden bridge of false teeth. The thing known as Enis Goddard clawed at the dental dam that masked its bare gums, and it flung the gilded prosthetic into the night. Membranes stretched taut as a pair of hooked fangs unhinged from the roof of its mouth. It lowered itself snarling, as gouts of venom ejaculated from its fangs, and dripped from the cusp of its chin.

The monster's single eye flicked in the direction of a hurtling mutt, as Yella Dog lunged with a guttural growl. The animal clamped its fangs into the folds of the creature's flaccid throat, thrashing its shaggy head from side to side. The boy sprung, Comanche arrow in hand, and he drove the shaft straight through the creature's chest, all the way to its turkey feather fletching.

The monster staggered backward, clawing at the wooden spike while the dog swung from its windpipe like an oversized necktie. Writhing, they collapsed coupled into the electrified nettles of barbed wire. Blue static spat from their intertwined bodies as the fairy lights descended upon them.

"Yella Dog!"

Black skies split beyond the electric blizzard. Both combatants were stilled by a white column of energy thick as a telephone pole. It dropped from the heavens to land upon the head of Enis Goddard. With a thunderclap so loud as to rattle every post for miles in its footing, one monster's life came to an end.

———◦—|◦—◦—|◦—◦—

The boy quit backfilling at first sight of Pap's Model T Tudor Sedan. He wiped his brow across his forearm, and stabbed his blade into the heap of soil. Using his hip as a fulcrum, he pitched a last scoop off the end of his spade. A last scoop to celebrate the end of another morning of toiling at a seemingly endless chore, and the beginning of what promised to be a bluebird afternoon.

The Model T rolled to a stop beside the boy's telephone pole. Pap squinted his eyes, looking the pole up and down as if he were on the verge of making some smart comment. His Pap still couldn't talk so very well, but it had made him a better listener, especially over their new telephone. He couldn't walk so very well either, not without a cane, but Pap sure loved to drive his Model T. It wasn't easy convincing Pap to sell the family land to invest in poles and augers, but in the end, Pap agreed that they'd made the best decision. Farming was finished. Their linemen's work had been good to them.

Yella Dog rose from her favorite spot on Pap's passenger seat when the boy approached the window. The mutt stretched and yawned with an ear-piercing whine, and then cocked her head to stare at the boy through her one good eye. After the lightning strike, Yella Dog couldn't walk much faster than Pap, but she sure liked to ride in a Model T. They made quite a pair, those two. No telling the odds that the both of them would take the hardest blow that Mother Nature could deal, right on the points of their chins, and then stand up and walk away. Seemed damned uncanny, and more than a little creepy, but if they were keeping some sort of a dark secret between them, they sure weren't telling. The boy guessed that it was alright if they were, and he guessed that there were more than a few dark secrets being guarded by those beneath their roof.

"M-Martha Cobb called," Pap said, wincing from the effort to stifle his stutter.

"Well, what'd she have to say?"

"She and J.P. are b-bringing over some rhubarb pie and l-lemonade."

"Well, that don't sound half bad," the boy said, squinting over his shoulder at the telephone pole he'd just set. "I'm about finished up, for now. It's about to start getting hot out. You got room for another passenger in there, or are you all full up?"

Pap's facial paralysis muted most expressions, but it heightened the effect of smiling eyes. Pap slid toward the center, allowing his son access to the driver's seat. He threw his arm around the furry shoulders of his favorite co-pilot. "S-slide your narrow ass on in here. You can drive us back home."

PART TWO OF SIX:

WHISPERS IN THE WIND

"Say, who's that down there on the road?" the boy whispered. "Ever seen him before?"

"By God, that's ol' Wandering Wesley," J.P. replied, grinning and squinting in the setting sun. "Boy, he sure has gotten old."

The bearded fellow limping down the dirt road was bent under the weight of a bulging burlap sack slung over one shoulder. Whatever was stuffed inside it emitted a muffled clatter with his every pendulous step. Looking more than a little bit like some aged sorcerer exiled from a faraway land, his arbitrary collection of mismatched clothing suggested that he'd been dressed, while napping, by a tizzy of mischievous fairies.

J.P. hallooed the strange traveler with a broad wave from the head of the driveway, but the fellow paid him no heed. Rather, he picked up his pace, muttering unintelligible nothings as he pressed toward the setting sun on his errand of wizardly significance.

J.P. chuckled. "That there's the last living son of Vorhees."

"Who's Vorhees?" The boy squinted in the tangerine light. "Can't say I ever heard of them."

"Ain't a who, it's a what. Vorhees was a town. Died nigh fifty years ago."

"A town can die?"

J.P. Cobb gave an almost imperceptible nod. "Darned right."

"How?"

J.P. spat into the dirt. "One of them old time diseases wiped them all out. Granddaddy called it Consumption. It was one of them maladies that never got properly understood before it vanished. Killed most everyone in that town before they ever knew what was happening."

"Where was Vorhees? Around here?"

"Yeah, between here and Rolla." J.P. fluttered his fingers at the sunset. "Probably where ol' Wandering Wesley's headed, if I don't miss my guess. That, or he's headed off to Rolla for tomorrow's big show."

"That's where Pap and I are headed, first thing tomorrow morning."

"That's what he told me. Going to see a drive, are ye?"

"Yep."

"Ever seen one before?"

"No, sir, but I'm sure looking forward to it."

"Going to whack a rabbit, are ye?"

The boy shrugged. "Maybe so. Reckon I'd better watch out, though. A lot of them old boys will probably be drunk, and swinging clubs."

J.P. gave a toothy grin, regarding the boy with twinkling amusement in his eyes. "I'd guess you're just exactly right about that." Chuckling, J.P. turned in the direction of the homestead, where the sweet-tart aroma of rhubarb pie wafted around the warm seam of the candlelit doorway. "Reckon we ought to go have us a slice of Martha's pie?"

The boy nodded and smiled. "I'd guess she'd be pretty sore if we didn't."

J.P. squeezed the boy's shoulder. Together, they quit their watch over the twilit road, and they made their way back up the gentle curve of the drive to the little home on the hillock where the boy and his Pap resided.

The homestead was pretty basic. It was just a rectangular, single-room situation, buried mostly into the earth. Only the tarpapered roof and the uppermost walls poked up above the ground, giving it a squat impression of something resembling a rabbit hutch, but you could stand up straight, inside. A sad garden loitered in the south yard. Beets hid under brine jars, beans under buckets. Their greens were mostly electrocuted by the static. Off to the west side was Mam's grave, occupying a quiet spot, all her own, where her thin, cedar cross jutted like a bowsprit toward the setting sun. Family shithouse was down the slope a piece.

Theirs was an older style of settlement, one appreciated for more than a century of prairie living for its low profile, and for its natural insulation that buffered the Kansas wind, bitter winters, and some measure of the dust. There was always going to be some dust that would find its way through every chink. Every morning, they awoke to the same fine, brown coating on everything. There was just no escaping it. Dust was just a condition of daily living.

After coming in from setting poles, the boy had washed up, and then he'd pulled some clean sheets over their mattresses. Couldn't say he'd ever felt embarrassed by a filthy pillow before, but for some reason, today he had. He'd swept a small hill of dust off the floor, pitched it out into the bare yard, and then he swept up a second one. By the time he'd finished fussing over their preparations for the evening company, he'd even set their table properly, with the small exception that their plates and glasses had to be placed upside-down, on account of the dust. The boy figured he'd wait to flip them over just before serving J.P. and Martha's food. Being fancy was kind of a pain in the ass, but he reckoned it was worth it. He didn't guess they'd used all them dishes since Mam was still alive. His eyes widened. That was a peculiar thought. On regular nights, he and Pap ate straight from the cookpot and lid. They sat shoulder to shoulder on the bench at their Osage table, quietly mouthing hambone and beans by oil light.

"Martha, your rhubarb pie was just real good," Pap said, dabbing his whiskers with a napkin. He leaned way back in his chair, and let out just a hiss of a burp.

Tonight, they'd enjoyed a real meal of roast chicken, with beets and taters in butter. All that, and some lemonade with rhubarb pie. Sometimes, life was so good you could just about taste it.

"Well, have you another slice of it." Martha Cobb was already up and serving it. "I don't want to have to take it home."

"Oh, dear Lord." Pap sighed, rubbing his hands over his swollen belly.

J.P. took up his mug, and he hoisted it aloft. "I'd like to propose a toast."

Martha noticed his movement even before he'd said a word, and her eyes seemed to brighten as she served a slice of pie. She whispered little frustrations when the slice clung to her pie knife, trying to slough its flaky crust and ruin itself. She poked it off, giggling mischievously, and sucked the dollop of pie filling off the end of her fingertip.

"I was telling Martha, I was afraid this dinner might not be the quite same without Darla. We miss her dearly, but you boys have sure done her proud. Here's to y'all."

The boy raised his cup. He glanced over at Pap, who'd flushed a little. Pap knuckled his mug with a halfhearted chuckle.

"I ain't trying to embarrass you, Lionel." J.P. rapped his thick fingertips against the table. "Here's to your retirement from farming, and to your lineman's contract. Now, if that ain't a proper toast then I don't know what is."

Pap glanced down into his mug. "All's I've got left to toast with is just a swig of buttermilk. Can a fellow toast with such a thing?"

J.P lowered his gaze, becoming serious. "I couldn't imagine a better drink to toast a retiring farmer with. Here's looking at you, Lionel Crow," J.P. winked at the boy, "and at you, as well."

Pap tipped his mug. "Thank ye kindly."

Martha cleared her throat. "Now, J.P. was trying to explain it all to me, how y'all got the contract to begin with, but I guess I just didn't understand it all."

Pap smeared away his buttermilk mustache. "Six months after Enis Goddard pulled his disappearing act, the Historical Guild went belly-up. They were the holders of the utility contract, not G-God."

"But God owned the Guild." Martha furrowed her brow. "He *was* the Guild, wasn't he?"

"Yes, ma'am. A whole lot of God's money was being laundered through there, you bet ye," Pap replied, with a knowing grin. "The Guild was G-God's invention, and his own private division our city government, but he never had a lawyer, so when he skinned out, the Guild went bankrupt, and the City of Eden had to go back out for bid on a contract that they technically held themselves. Try and w-wrap your head around that one, why don't ye."

"Well, that just don't seem right."

"Well, it wasn't right!" J.P. interjected. "There wasn't nothing in Eden that has been what it's seemed for about as long as I can remember, and that's largely because of Enis Goddard."

"And I wasn't selling no easement to that son-of-a-bitch, but I was happy to pick up his defaulted contract. Not much anyone could say in disagreement. Without my say-so, wasn't nobody getting any closer to L-Liberal than God ever did."

"Like you always told me, Pap, if you take good care of a section of land, then that land will take care of you," the boy said, gazing up at Pap, "but I'll bet you never figured on it taking care of us this way."

"N-no, I sure didn't. I hated to sell it, but it was the right thing to do."

"I'd say you're right," Martha said, forking up a bite of pie, and covering her mouth. "You boys are just about finished with your line to Liberal, aren't you?"

"Just about," Pap said, sighing and rubbing his eyes. "We'll have steady work through the summer, for sure, but we can't be dragging our feet if we hope to pick up a contract for that second leg, from Eden to Rolla. If them Mormon ruins standing in the way ever go to probate, we'll be waiting to snatch them up."

"Shiloh Swales—isn't that what those ruins are called?"

"Yes'm. That's how God's Historical Guild got their hooks into the contract to begin with. It was always about running a phone line from Liberal to Rolla, but God owned them ruins, and all the land around them. Only he could run that line, and he knew it."

"He was a smart one," J.P. said, "I'll give him that. Just as smart as the devil himself. Sumbitch though he could buy off anybody."

"Buy or threaten, one." Pap shot a glance at the boy, who dropped his eyes to his plate, where his fork muddled a goober of pie filling.

"Any word on where ol' God run off to?"

Pap shook his head.

"Ain't that strange? Ain't it just strange that he'd just up and disappear like that?"

The boy kept his head lowered. His eyes remained trained on his plate, where his fork pushed the blob of rhubarb around the edge until it had bled completely out of crimson sauce. He couldn't wait until the subject of Enis Goddard would quit coming up in conversations, but he guessed that it was going to be quite a while. God's sudden disappearance was perhaps the best gossip that the Eden community had enjoyed for as long as the boy could remember. Seemed that way to him, anyhow.

Pap shrugged. "Plenty of folks have skinned out over the years."

"I know it, but God? Lord knows he had the staying power, and his roots here ran much deeper than mine. His people was Mormon, ye know. Them old dugouts at Shiloh Swales? The Goddard family has got some history there. You bet ye."

"What happened," the boy asked, clearing his throat, fawning across the table at J.P., "to all them Mormons?"

Pap's eyes flicked up from his plate, and immediately narrowed. "What would make you think that something *happened* to them? Somebody been telling you stories, have they?"

J.P. finished his buttermilk, set down his mug, and exhaled through his teeth. By the candlelight, there didn't look to be any whites to his eyes. Just stars reflecting in a couple of dark puddles. "Y'know, history gets written by the winners. Look back through all your books, and all you ever read about are the folks who were successful, the ones who survived the winters, the diseases, and all the barbarian hordes. Seldom ye hear a word about the colonies that failed. Shiloh Swales was one of those."

"Reckon it was one of them old diseases that got 'em? Like what happened in Vorhees? Consun ... Comsun ..."

"Consumption?" J.P. said, and shrugged. "I suspect what happened in Shiloh Swales was a damned sight worse than that. Something violent." He rocked back and forth on his chair legs, just watching the flames of the candles dance atop their wicks. "My great-granddaddy was called on to try and help them out of their situation. He and his son went out there together. I'd guess his son—my grand-daddy—was probably about your age when they done it. How old are ye?"

"'Levin."

"Maybe a touch older than that." J.P. Cobb sucked his teeth and looked up to the ceiling. "My great-granddaddy was what ye might call a strong-armed abolitionist. He done some pretty mean favors in his time for a number of causes that he believed in, including the cause of those Mormon squatters."

"Why?" The boy straightened up in his seat, furrowing his brow. "Was he a Mormon?"

"No, and he wasn't colored, neither. But sticking up for them people was just what Great-Granddaddy Cobb believed in, and he was willing to fight and kill for it. Killed a lot of men over his beliefs. To tell a family secret, he's the assassin who shot and killed ol' Lyndon Boggs."

"Lyndon Boggs?" The boy glanced from J.P. to Pap and back again. "Who's that?"

"Never mind. Point is, my Great-Granddaddy was a protective sort. Nothing was more important to him than family, and that included other families who looked to be in trouble. The Shiloh Swales situation was a particularly bad one. Whatever Great-Granddaddy seen out there changed him for life."

"What'd he see?"

J.P. let his chair legs down to rest. "Most likely the Indians had got to them. That would be my guess. But the Goddard family was one amongst those he went to rescue, so I suppose you can thank me and my family line for preserving God's. Guess I owe everyone an apology."

"No, you don't," Pap replied.

"It all worked out for the best," the boy said, "in the end."

After a long spell of candlelit silence, J.P. let his hand fall onto Martha's thigh with a soft smack. He spoke without ever opening his eyes. "Well, dear. Don't you think we'd better let these boys get to bed? They've got an awful big day, tomorrow."

"Oh? What plans have you got?"

The boy's eyes brightened. "We're headed out to Rolla, first thing in the morning. Aren't we, Pap? Gonna see my first rabbit drive!"

⁘

Sundried snakes rattled stiff and strange along the fencerow. A human funnel trudged the dunes beyond. Ruddy winds came boiling and spinning over the stubble until the Last Man's Club was enveloped in a cloud of dust. Clutching masks, twisting their spines to the scouring winds, they disappeared for a full minute. When at last the filth dissipated, men were doubled-over and retching, reeling from the blast, but they did not break their formation.

The duster receded, trailing its slithering tendrils of silt past the ranks of mummified rattlesnakes. A gathered crowd numbering more than a thousand released a cheer as the drivers resumed their march. Onlookers pushed goggles up over their filthy foreheads. They lowered their dust masks to their chins, exposing nostrils plugged and glistening with Vaseline. Jugs of corn whiskey were in motion, passed hand-to-hand throughout the crowd.

Safely upwind of the barbeque pits, the Rainmaker perched atop a flatbed with a bullhorn pressed to his face. He directed his crew with a sweeping rod that dictated precise placement of his ordnance. Cases of shells were being stacked near the breeches of three army howitzers that stood charged and aimed for the heavens. Downwind, a potluck band of cowboy strings, Rolla brass and a Rooshian accordion were setting stage. Musicians tuned their instruments in a billowing cloud of mesquite.

"L-look right out there. See? They're headed right for the pen." Pap pointed a quavering finger in a direction where the earth itself appeared to be retreating the advancing funnel of drivers. The ground seemed to churn against the fencerow in rippling heaves of dust and fur.

"How many you figure they're going to catch?" the boy asked.

"Couple thousand, I'd reckon."

"Couple *thousand*?"

Pap licked the grit from his teeth. "When you was just a baby, your mam and I once seen them drive six-thousand rabbits off this very same field."

A few of the creatures had already entered the corral, two hundred yards ahead of the drivers. They loped demurely about, as they explored the perimeter of the enclosure. They didn't seem to be alarmed, not yet. They reared up on their hind legs to inflict curious nibbles to the chicken wire fence. They swiveled their cornhusk ears, gawping back at the encroaching rabbit stampede before the drivers. Despite the imminent threat, some dropped back to all fours to graze demurely in the wheat stubble. Maybe gnawing was a nervous habit, or maybe they were just dumb. It was hard to get inside the head of a jackrabbit.

Just as the band struck up the first chord of "Stormy Weather," one farmer staggered forth from the line of onlookers to address the crowd with a sweep of his jug, and a bellow that bubbled with dust pneumonia. "Here they come! Start squeezing up on them, folks! Start squeezing up!" The flank was in motion. The whole crowd marched toward the fencerow, closing the walls of the trap. The entire mass of rabbits seemed at once to understand their predicament, but their realization had come but a minute too late. Panic forced a rude divide, inspiring the leading half to rush maniacally into the corral, while the trailing portion attempted a mindless retreat back toward the drivers. The fastest runners were first to collide with sticks and swinging chains. They reversed direction, only to meet headlong with a second wave of rabbits that had just appraised the enclosure as a promise of certain death.

Blocked to the south by the fence festooned with dried rattlesnakes, to the north by the wall of drunken revelers, the creatures became crazed with fright. They poured in their thousands into the enclosure, where they performed wild leaps into the air.

"Close 'er up! Close 'er up!"

A few seasoned wranglers dragged a gate behind the corralled animals and quickly fastened it with bailing wire. Inside, rabbits attacked each other. Naturally timid creatures bore leather punch incisors, tearing back red flags of hide with vicious kicks from their hind claws. Many forced their conical heads through holes in the chicken wire to strangle like fish in a gill net, eyes rolling, red mouths gasping.

Drivers leapt in over the gate. Crowds pressed around the teeming corral to cheer every blow with the bloodlust of spectators at an amphitheater. Flailing chains bejeweled their filthy faces with slung gore. Clubs rose and fell in terrific arcs, punctuated by dull thuds and agonized squeals. Clobbered accidentally in the chops, one driver clutched his ruined mouth as he fell growling into the rabbits.

The young children's initial excitement devolved into horror. One by one, they relaxed their grip on the chicken wire enclosure, turning away from the terrible melee. One after another ran bawling into the wastelands. Even at fifty yards distance, and despite the band's champing brass, there was no escape the squealing thousands of massacred rabbits. One toddler's tears tilled pale rows down her cheeks as she clasped her ears and danced, as if to the asthmatic braying of a nearby accordion. Her little mouth hung agape in an unheard scream.

"I ain't going to lie to you, folks. I'm going to make one hell of a ruckus here in Rolla!" The voice of the Rainmaker resounded over the crowd. "But what you're bound to lose in sleep over the next three days and nights, you'll soon be measuring in inches." The Rainmaker lowered his bullhorn to nod and grin, as he paced the deck of his flatbed. He raised the bullhorn again, engaging the gathering crowd with his politician's talent for making the same dubious promise a hundred different ways.

Most folks had left the rabbit corral to edge closer to loiter around the Rainmaker's platform, mostly discussing matters unrelated to the business of busting clouds. This character wasn't the first to try and sell his dubious science to the residents of the High Plains. Others had come before him, flying kites laden with dynamite, releasing gas-filled balloons. Whatever their methodology, they were always quick with their excuses when their meddling with the skies failed to produce any rain.

This go-around, it was the Rainmaker's use of army howitzers that prompted the Last Man's Club and Rolla's chamber of commerce to pass the hat. Not that anyone had much faith that this latest clown was apt to squeeze any water from the sky. Rather, it was their interest in the army howitzers. They were bound to be a crowd pleaser. Any entertainment to create a buzz was liable to whip up a sense of community across the broken and barren lands. Rolla was the end of the line. It was the gateway to the dead corner of Kansas. If ever there were ever a place needing a big boost in morale, Rolla was it.

Once the Rainmaker was booked, the mayor organized a rabbit drive, a town barbeque, and a street dance. Wasn't long before some banker took notice of the promise of activity, and further sweetened the pot by adding a farm foreclosure auction to the itinerary. The Rooshian accordion players brought a following of German mackerel-crackers out of Liberal, all eager to dance the Hochzeit. They rolled into Rolla in a train of mule-drawn wagons laden with kegs of warm beer, adding the pungent odor of boiled cabbage to clouds of burning mesquite. In the end, the Rainmaker was all but lost in the storm of activity he'd inadvertently seeded, but since his fee was of course collected in advance, being upstaged was a moot point.

Barbequed jackrabbit and watermelon filled plates between the Rainmaker's speech and the street dance, which was scheduled for sundown. Most of the farmers ate standing around the auctioneer, calling bids while they gnawed rabbit hinds. A red-faced banker seized the bull-horn after a second tractor went for a dime, but his threats to bring in his own bidders only brought jeers and flung watermelon rinds. Foreclosure auctions belonged to the Last Man's Club. The bankers had only just begun to get wise to the farming network that fixed bids, muscled out competition. Only thing worse than a jackrabbit was a damned banker. A rabbit, at least, you could barbeque.

"Well, how-do, Lionel Crow! How's things going on the line?"

Pap rose from where he'd been sitting in the dirt alongside a bunch of farmers taking turns on a jug. He wiped his palm on his trousers, and shook hands with a fellow dressed in green overalls and a red shirt, whose rotund body resembled a watermelon. "L-looking awful good." Pap threw his arm around the boy's shoulders. "We're fixing to run our last stretch to the county line."

"All your poles set to Liberal, are they?"

"D-darned near. Been hard at it, me and my boy."

The man winked at the boy. "Been helping your Pap set them poles, have you?"

"Shoot, he's done most of the work." Pap jostled the boy's shoulder, and smiled down at him. "I ain't been worth a shit since Black Sunday."

"Looks like Mother Nature will have to swat you harder next time, won't she?"

"S-sure hope not. I'd say once was enough."

The man laughed until a wad of black sputum came up. He grimaced, cocked his head, and lobbed it into the dirt. The boy couldn't help but stare at the spot where it landed with a puff of dust.

Seemed like everyone west of Eden showed signs of dust pneumonia. The air was worse out here, filled with gritty ash that tickled the lungs and made the boy want to cough with every breath. He'd seen some folks coughing up blood. Nothing grew here. Livestock went blind, and babies stopped breathing in the night. Nothing but bad news ever came from out this way. Even the air had a sickly smell, apart from the Rooshian cabbage. The boy frowned at the dunes of drifted dust slumped against the south side of every structure. Made him wonder if the fate of Rolla would one day be the same as Vorhees.

"Well, I don't aim to trouble you on your day off, Lionel, but you come see me next week about the paperwork, and we'll start pulling some lines." The man coughed into his handkerchief, wiped his lip, and then jammed the wadded rag into the back pocket of his overalls. He reached out to tousle the boy's hair. "Don't give your Pap too much trouble now, you hear?"

"No, sir."

Pap watched as the watermelon-shaped man limped away. Then, he turned to the boy. "Had you had a chance to meet him, yet?"

"No. When would I have?"

"Thought maybe he'd come around while you was working."

"No."

"He's an agent backing our contract. He was backing the City of Eden before they went bankrupt, and now he's backing us." Pap pulled a swig off a passed jug.

"You mean he was backing the damned Historical Guild?"

"Son, I don't know what you're all addled about."

"He was probably a friend of Enis Goddard," the boy said, kicking the dirt.

"What exactly do you mean, 'was' a friend?" Pap narrowed his eyes at the boy.

The boy felt all the blood in his head drop right through a trap door in his chest. "I didn't mean nothing by it. Ain't nobody seen him around, is all."

42

Pap stared at the boy. "Got a lot of big worries for a boy your age."

"Come on, Pap." The boy sighed. "S'pose something happened to you. Say you got struck by lightning again, I got to learn about all this stuff so I'd at least know how to keep the business."

"Once we get that cable strung, you won't need to know how to do nothing but pick up a monthly check. Think you can handle that?"

"I just don't get why for years you wouldn't part with that strip of easement God wanted, because you hated to see a rich man get richer, but first chance you get you run off and line the pockets of some banker who was most likely a friend of God's."

"I never said he was a goddamned banker." Pap lowered his jug and stared hard at the boy. "I don't know what's crawled up your ass, but as l-long as they shell out our annuities, I reckon our investor can be friends with anyone he damned well pleases. It's our contract, not his, and besides, there's just going to be some things in this world that you don't need to know. Not now and not ever! You got that?"

"I guess."

Pap handled the financial end of the contract, while the boy handled the shovel. Not that the boy was at all interested in percentages and annuities and so forth, but the vagaries inherent in the way Pap always handled everything could be aggravating as hell if he allowed himself to stew over all that he wasn't trusted to know.

"What do you mean, you guess?"

The boy shot a glance up at Pap, already anxious over the nice straight answer that he wasn't bound to get. "Just sounds like we're roped into something bigger than you want to let on."

"Course we are. That's how the world works, but it's all just government money, at the end of the day."

"That don't make no sense."

"You like to keep things simple, do ye? Well, then look at it this way: you and me, we're l-landlords, and them telephone poles are our tenants. Monthly annuity checks are our rent. Best of all, when the rest of them Goddard easements all go off to foreclosure, there's bound to be a big ol' auction, and you can bet your britches that the Last Man's Club is going to be waiting."

This time, it was the boy who narrowed his eyes at Pap. "What do mean *'when'* the Goddard easements go to foreclosure?"

Pap winked. "I just mean that ain't nobody seen Enis around lately, that's all."

The boy took a fistful of Pap's shirt, and leaned against him. "There's still a lot more I ought to know about."

"C-come on," Pap said, nudging the boy with his elbow. "Let's go on over to the dance. Maybe we can find you a girlfriend who'll help me keep you busy."

Blushing, the boy turned in step with Pap, who teetered badly as he tossed a gnawed rabbit bone to the ground. The boy glanced quizzically up at his father. Pap very seldom drank. Next to never. He supposed it was better if Pap drank for happy occasions like tonight than for sad ones, because Lord knew they'd had enough of those come to pass. The grip of Pap's hand tightened on the back of his neck. The boy crooked his head to see what had brought them to a halt, and when what was rising up into the sky, he sucked a gritty gasp of Rolla air.

They spewed skyward as a solid column, black against the setting sun. Diverging at the apex, they branched outward across the horizon in a great fan of writhing streamers. The shape of a black locust tree unfurled across the fiery sky. Although they were many miles to the west, the boy could feel their collective presence, and it was a presence that chilled him to the marrow.

Bats.

On clear summer evenings when the dust wasn't so thick, he liked to watch them loop through the sky, but he often found himself wondering where they came from. The High Plains weren't exactly known for their caves. There were no mountains, hills, canyons, no structures of any kind. There weren't even any hollow trees. Nothing but hundreds of square miles of the same flat, featureless windblown plains racing to the horizon in every direction. There was the fountainhead, before him. It looked as if there was a rip in the wasteland through which those millions of creatures spewed, a gaping portal straight to Hell, out in the heart of no man's land.

As the boy gawped up at the dark legion, he imagined each bat as being one soul of every life lost to this godforsaken desert since time's beginning, and it had in fact claimed many. There was a bat for every one of them. A bat for bygone friends. A bat for the mother he mourned. A bat for every life lost in eras harsher than this one. Gone, but not forgotten. Although their windows of time had closed, the boy could sense the rapping of their million fingertips against the pane. How thick was the glass that kept a million souls from spilling out of one era, and into the next? Was there any glass at all?

The boy's gaze fell from the skies to land upon a wizardly character slinking through the crowds. The old crone glanced furtively over his shoulder at the bat volcano, knotting his snowy beard in both hands, as if the growth had sprouted overnight and he'd just discovered it. A stethoscope swung from his spindly neck. A collection of nameless fitments stuffed into his sack all jangled with his every step like a strange instrument for his one-man band.

"Wandering Wesley," the boy whispered.

A watermelon rind cartwheeled through the air, and smacked the old hermit in the back of the head. He spun around, chest heaving, eyes searching. A shrill peal of laughter came from a nearby gang of kids.

"There they go. There they go." Wandering Wesley jabbed his gnarled finger at the swarming skies. "Amen! Let's get on back now. Get on back while the getting's good."

"Be sure and write us once you get there, Wesley," a drunken farmer bellowed, knuckling his buddy's arm. The hermit pivoted at the waist without ever breaking stride, and snapped a salute at his antagonists. A great belt of laughter erupted from that section of the crowd. More than a few salutes were returned.

The boy frowned at the unruly crowd. He reckoned a lot of these farmers had been making sport of poor Wesley since they were children, as if the Vorhees orphan was nothing more than a divine gift to a land starved for laughter. Seemed like Wandering Wesley had it worse than anybody.

"Does he still live in Vorhees, Pap?" the boy asked.

"Well, Vorhees ain't so much a town as a geographical l-location." Pap hiccupped, leaning heavily on the boy for support. "Hell, we passed it just this morning."

46

"We did?"

"Few clicks p-past them Mormon ruins, south of the sand draw out there on the dead section."

The boy strained to pull up an image of the old site, which amounted to not much more than a quarter-mile of different weed varieties than what normally grew in the surrounding fields. He recalled an old windmill pad, maybe some scattered rubble.

"That's it?"

"Yep." Pap spat. "Land fails, businesses fail, walls crumble and wood rots."

"You ever gone out there and poked around?"

Pap cleared his throat, and licked his lips. "Can't recall, if I ever did. Ain't nothing to see."

"S'pose Wandering Wesley is going out there, to-night?"

"Hard telling, with that one." Pap chuckled, and pulled a swig from a jug handed to him. He thanked the donor kindly, and passed it back. "But there ain't nothing out there. So don't go getting any bright ideas."

The boy frowned up at Pap. What an odd thing to say. Probably still fuming over him breaking into the old school house, poking through that cedar trunk, swiping that damned quiver of arrows. Pap had lost a great deal of trust in him over that. Might not ever fully trust him again, and it was aggravating that he could never tell Pap how one of those stolen arrows had saved his life.

Wandering Wesley crouched to light a small lantern. He rose again and loped out of Rolla until the music of his jangling sack was absorbed by the potluck band. At the edge of town, the old fool twirled around to perform some parting gesture that a number of drunks were all waiting to imitate. The boy watched disapprovingly as the staggering throngs began to mock him, incorporating lewd gestures into their various reenactments. Wandering Wesley didn't seem to mind. In fact, it was difficult to tell if his strange signals were even meant for the howling audience, or if he was communicating with something else, something far beyond the crowds of Rolla.

Everyone flattened as a thunderous fusillade resonated through the earth. The band stopped, and a few women screamed. Bats looped through a flash of sparkling cordite that bedazzled the evening sky. A tremendous cheer arose. All heads, drunk and sober, swiveled in the direction of the Rainmaker's platform, where a gun-blue plume of smoke rolled from the barrel of a skyward howitzer.

"Lordy!" Pap said, his hand rising to his chest.

Bellowed demands for another shelling emanated throughout the crowd, while wailing children cowered with their hands clamped over their ears. They'd probably never sleep right again, after all they'd seen and heard today. The Rainmaker was strutting atop his flatbed, bullhorn in hand, while the other hand gently tamped the air in an effort to still the crowd. He appeared to have reclaimed his hijacked show. While his crew scurried to charge the cannons, the Rainmaker recommenced to bloviating on the science of busting clouds, citing indisputable evidence that dated back to the Napoleonic Wars. Somewhere, a bottle shattered. Women gathered distraught children, ushering them back toward the festival's darkening edge, where a harvest moon was cresting the bat-spangled sky.

<hr />

"Here, you get his legs. I got this end." A faceless farmer slipped beneath Pap's arms, hugging him around the breadbasket. Pap's head wagged around like a fermented apple on its stem. His boot heels plowed ruts in the dust, until another couple of farmers each grabbed a leg, and hoisted Pap up off the ground. Together, they staggered toward the Model T. One of his handlers lost footing, and fell face-first into Pap's lap just as they plunked him down in the passenger seat. They all howled over that one for longer than the boy thought it was funny. Eventually, a farmer reached in to give Pap a loving pat on the head, and then, he slammed the door. Pap lilted to the right until his cheek was pressed against the window.

"You take good care of your Pap, now." One of the men reached out for the boy's head, but missed completely. He stumbled into the fender of the Model T. This inspired another long spell of laughter that the boy couldn't wait to subside. He thanked the strangers flatly, and then walked around to the driver's seat. He slammed the door, and looked over at Pap, who was already starting to snore. Sometimes, respect for Pap came so easily. Other times, the boy had to try hard to convince himself that his father wasn't just an old fool. He cursed under his breath, as they rolled off the fairgrounds, and out onto the road.

The drive from Rolla to Eden felt kind of like traversing the surface of the moon. The road could scarcely be defined from the enveloping desolation. At times, the boy had to apply the brakes and squint to determine if he was still on track. The thought of accidentally running off the road and purring clear out into the wastelands always triggered a gush of terror that surged up through his chest and sharpened his mind. He tightened his grip on the wheel. Out here, a fellow could drive in circles until his automobile ran out of fuel, and he'd not likely ever find the missing road again. Even by the light of day, you could drive forever in the wrong direction without ever hitting another road.

The boy's anger with Pap over pickling himself was chilled by anxiety. Beyond losing the road, the boy's greatest fear would be having to explain that screw-up to Pap, if the old man woke hung over and dehydrated to find that they were lost in the middle of a desert. Few fates were more terrifying than that of looking like an idiot in the eyes of your father.

The boy slowed the Model T, and stared out over the road. There was a sort of pattern becoming apparent that he hadn't noticed before. Regular pocks in the moon dust, one after another, like footprints. The boy's emotions oscillated between worry and relief, since the new trail gave him something to follow, at least, but he knew that there was no guarantee that whoever had left them had managed to keep to the road. Just as likely, the tracks would lead him straight out into the heart of the old Comancheria, where tramps danced with flittering bats, and crooned to their hermit gods.

There was a light up ahead. Damned if it wasn't a lantern. Another flare of panic whistled up through the boy's core, as he searched the ring of lantern light for its owner, but he saw no one in the vicinity. He stopped the Model T, breathing heavily, and stared at the lonely beacon. Beside him, Pap snored away like an old hog. Even if he could roust him from his sleep, drunk as he was, there wasn't a damned landmark from here to Kingdom Come. Waking him up would be like removing someone's blindfold in some random spot of land that didn't look any different than anyplace else in three-hundred miles. Didn't matter how well you thought you knew this country, where roads created a false sense of familiarity. This was a barren land that could revert itself in an instant to the death trap that it always had been, and always would be.

The boy cursed, thumping his fist against the wheel. He guessed he could always follow his own tire tracks back to Rolla, if the blowing dust hadn't already filled them. The boy released his foot from the brake. He pushed the throttle lever forward, easing the automobile closer to the glowing lantern. As he rolled into the ring of lantern light, he discerned a dark lump to be Wandering Wesley's burlap sack, resting near a row of weeds.

"Well, where the hell did you go?"

The boy scanned the periphery for any sign of the old loony bird, wherever the hermit might be grousing behind a shock of moonlit weeds. To the left, the angles and straight edges of a man-made form, low against the ground, produced a stark contrast to the fluid drifts of dust. It was the base of an old windmill pad.

"Vorhees."

It brought some relief to feel his fragmented mental maps rushing back into a recognizable form. The boy looked around at the stands of ragweed and sage, and he knew that there would be a draw deep enough to swallow a Model T just beyond those weeds. That put the missing road forty yards to the right, a direction he now knew to be south. His world was coming back together.

The boy closed his eyes and drew a deep breath. He released it in a long and pleasurable exhale, but the breath caught in his chest when he saw the thing at the edge of the clearing, where a fat moth fluttered in the ragweed. There were two of them, jutting bluntly from the dust like a couple of thin piers that once supported a missing structure, but they weren't piers, as nice and normal as that might've been. They were shins. Capped by ragged knobs of flesh, splintered bone, they were all that remained of whomever had been snapped clean off of their standing feet, and was spirited away into the night.

PART THREE OF SIX:

BLEEDING KANSAS

Dust hung thin as a funeral shroud over the pale harvest moon. Must have been a little of that moonlight magic that brought hoodwinks to Clapboard Row. Crouching in the shadows, the boy inhaled a lungful of the warm night air. It was an unusually bright one, tonight—a perfect night for reading.

Pap had slept off his hangover until noon. Then, he'd stepped outside, got sick, and spent the hotter part of afternoon down at the windmill. When he finally returned, sopping from his daylong bath, he crawled right into bed without supper. There'd not been not a moment to discuss the previous evening's events, not that the boy felt much like admitting that he'd accidentally driven into Vorhees, and what terrible thing he'd seen when he got there. The questions raised by what exactly had happened to Wandering Wesley were just sorts of questions that Pap was loathe to answer, but he was starting to think that maybe he didn't need Pap much anymore. At least, not when it came to solving the case of the terrible secret that Enis Goddard had been keeping from their community.

Even with his death, something of God's threat seemed to linger. There were missing pages to his story. Whole chapters. Things like Enis don't just happen overnight, and as for poor Wesley, the only thing the boy could say for certain was that his days of wandering were over. Until he learned the truth, the whole of it, the ghost of Enis Goddard would continue to whisper in the wind. For the sake of his own sanity, he needed some closure on the subject.

The boy didn't move a muscle. He watched as the faceless custodian stood exposed and awash in the cool effervescence. The old fellow limped along with his nightly duties, snuffing all the gas lights along the boardwalk. He appeared no larger than an insect beneath the windmill jutting from the town square like a great steel sunflower. Rotating blades squealed and groaned in the nightly breeze, as though it pained the machine to lose the irregular spurts of water that gushed from its severed stem. The custodian's boots rippled puddles left behind by volunteer firemen. A few hours ago, they'd come through town and rolled their pumper the length of Main, spraying down the dust that coated Eden's main artery until the street shimmered in the moonlight like a Cimarron tributary.

Drawn and standing water in such abundance was a portentous sight in a place where it had for ages been the last word imparted by cracked lips of countless folks who'd attempted to cross the Great American Desert. But in a spirit of irony so cruel that only Mother Nature could have conceived of such a thing, cool and boundless grottos of water were hidden just thirty feet beneath the blasted crust. The largest body of fresh water in the whole danged country, if not the world, had remained untapped since time's beginning. The Ogallala Aquifer, they were calling it. Once that subterranean ocean was discovered, windmills began tapping the High Plains just like a swarm of bloodsucking skeeters.

Out in the middle of the square, the steel sunflower moaned and released another gush. Stolen droplets of the earth's lifeblood bejeweled every hitching post and lantern, leaving Main Street drenched as a slaughterhouse floor.

The custodian sidled up to the windmill's base. He removed his hat and hung it on the nub of a crossbeam. He bent, and with both hands, dipped into the sparkling essence that filled the public tank. As he washed, a strange animal, maybe a raccoon, slipped soundlessly through the backdrop, fading in and out of existence along forever's black and muted edge. So engrossed was he in the rare pleasure of washing, the custodian never took notice of the furry critter ambling across the road. Nor had he noticed the boy, skulking behind the creamery, studying the custodian with stars in his eyes.

He moved when the custodian moved. He stopped when the custodian stopped. Sliding catlike through the gloom behind Clapboard Row, the boy appeared in instants between stores, then vanished again into tussocks of pigweed. He certainly appeared to know precisely where he was going, as though he'd had travelled this route before, perhaps at this same time of night with the same single purpose.

The custodian rose dripping from the trough. He turned, and the boy dropped to his belly in the dry grass, stilling a chorus of crickets. The custodian stared in the direction of the new silence for some time, and then whipped around toward the movement of a raccoon that he'd just noticed waddling in the street. Retrieving his hat, he pinched the water from his nose, slicked back his wetted hair, then plunked his hat back into place. He then commenced to limping on down the flooded avenue, killing lights, one at a time. The boy watched him, waiting until his outline dissolved into the night. A cricket resumed its chirping, at arm's length.

The schoolhouse was closed, and not just for the day. He'd once attended school there, but the best lessons he guessed he'd ever taken from that place were the ones he'd swiped long after its doors were closed, after the Historical Guild took possession and nailed boards over its windows. Seemed like the Guild took an interest in a whole lot of things around town that didn't have much historical value. Eden had always struck him as being peculiar in that way. Sometimes seemed as though a phantom agenda with a life all its own had forever crept through town, sucking up things in its path like a great slug through table scraps. The head of that slug seemed to be the Historical Guild, and it was no surprise that the Guild's chairman was none other than Enis Goddard. Well, had been, anyway. A shiver coursed up the boy's spine.

J.P. liked to say that history gets written by the winners, and in Kansas, the winners were the Free Staters. They were folks who prevailed over the Missouri slavers, the Indians, the Yankee Mormons, and every other variety of character who'd been squatting out there in No Man's Land while history was being written. Abolitionists wrote the books, so any alternate perspectives on Eden's queer heritage had since been reduced to hearsay. In fact, the only evidence in existence that Eden had risen from the ashes of a lost colony of slaughtered Mormons was the stuff locked away inside a certain cedar trunk.

Why the Historical Guild had seized the trunk of journals from J.P.'s family, around sixty years ago, was one of those questions the elders seemed loathe to answer. J.P. would have been about the boy's own age when the Guild stormed his family farmhouse, and dragged that trunk out into the yard. The violence of that night had so shaken J.P. that he'd locked the reasons behind it away, and no amount of whiskey and watermelon had yet to produce the key. However, a good hammer would always do the job, wherever a key was lacking.

"I'm sorry, Pap," the boy whispered, as he sprung the lock on the school house door with a dull clank.

This Fine Collection of Indian Artifacts, Letters and Journals were Graciously Donated to the Eden Historical Guild by the Cobb Family.

DUST TO DUST

[Contents of trunk's upper tray: Comanche bow, quiver, nine arrows and beaded breastplate; assorted vials, tins and apothecary jars; assorted cookware and ordinary fitments.]

[Contents of trunk's lower compartment: letters and bound leather journals in varying conditions, chronologically organized.]

[from the diary of Early Goddard, aged 12]

11 March, 1857

Ada got stung by a rattlesnake in her sleep. Mam and Papa loaded her in the wagon and set off for Brother Merrick's. He is no sort of doctor, but in his care his eldest daughters were spared the Consumption that took his boys, so we pray he should have some good medicine against snakes. There have been many snakes about our dugouts since thaw. This morning Enis and I set about killing heaps of them. We strung them up at the field's edge as gifts for the Indians. We pray they should like these snakes and see fit to leave us be, for it's still too dangerous go into the fields. Look at little Enis waiting now at the latch hole with a carving knife. He wants more than anything to cut off an Indian finger.

[Letter from Marshall Goddard to Mormon President Brigham Young]

24 March, 1857

58

M. C. NORRIS

Dear President and Brother Young:

*I Marshall Goddard of Shiloh Swales am husband
to Luretia, am father to Ada aged nineteen, am father
to Early and Enis aged twelve and seven. I served in
battle against the Missouri Militia at Haun's Mill and
there I was wounded in the legs and face. I am one of
your Crooked River Boys.*

*I write for your blessed permission to abandon this
place. Here the Indians are riled over a border dispute
along the Cheyenne Strip. Here many are killed. Here
we suffer Consumption, Indians and rattlesnakes. My
beloved daughter Ada is stung. I enclose a lock of her
yellow hair. Indians keep us from our fields, from
hunting, from gathering chips and water. Here my
children starve. Here my Brothers die. [illegible due to
mold] a doctor, and as many young men of fighting age
as can be mustered, or none in Shiloh Swales shall be
spared by the year's end.*

I beg you like a dog for leave.

M. Goddard

⸻

*[Letter from unidentified author, presumably Mormon
President Brigham Young, to Dr. Beauregard "Buckshot"
Cobb of Lawrence, Kansas]*

G.S.L. City, Oct 17, 1857

*Doctor Beauregard Cobb
Lawrence, Kansas*

Dear Friend:

Forgive me that I should trouble you with a fue lines, but so rare are fighting surgeons, and rarer still with hearts good as yours yet spared to serve God in their noble capacity. I remember verry well your valor in the Missouri Wars, and your sympathy toward my Brothers at Crooked River and Haun's Mill.

I hear with great pleasure that you remain the same Angel in hospital and Devil incarnate in battle that I so fondly remember from the old days, still a doctoring our friends and a warring our common enemies in Lawrence and Pottawatomie. You and your Abolitionists are truly God's divine hand, poised to halt the spread of evil unto His prairies and plains. Forgive me that I venture to write you more fully than I deem prudent, with post offices and mail bags meeting close inspection, but I trust in my Indian couriers that this letter shall safely find you.

I trouble you with news of a second front along the Cimarron, where the Missouri Devils have slipped out into western Kansas Territory. There, a fort is under construction by their squatters' assembly. War must be delivered swiftly unto them before they soon stake their claims and begin to bully the ballot boxes. Please let those with ears heed this warning!

In dangerous proximity to this slaving fort lies a secret colony of my Brothers called Shiloh Swales. Apart from my Self, none outside this remote settlement has been made to know of its existence, for the threat upon Mormon lives has never been so great. The tragedy at Mountain Meadows has wrought such profound hatred of the "Yankee Mormon" that not the least of my Brothers would I chance to send across the Utah border.

Every trail is imperiled by our opposition, eager to cut down my Brothers wherever they find them.

I enclose a recent letter written me by our dear Friend and Brother, Marshall Goddard of Shiloh Swales, whose name you shall recall from the massacre at Haun's Mill. Inside this letter is a lock of yellow hair cut from the head of poor Ada, Brother Goddard's eldest daughter. I forward this sad evidence to you, that you should be made aware of this good family's terrible suffering. Please keep this clipped bit of the girl at all times close to your breast, until such time as you should be inspired to reunite it with her ailing whole.

I beg you send a rescue party to this family, Dr. Cobb, and to any other families at Shiloh Swales yet spared. Disguise your party as a train of common homesteaders to best shepherd our lost flock back to your Free State stronghold in Lawrence until, God willing, popular hatred of Mormons abates. For this favor, I advance you the sum of five hundred dollars for fresh horses and provisions, and I will reward you a hundred dollars more for every Mormon head spared. Whether you accept or decline, do not send any reply. Consider the five hundred dollars compensation for your service to our Church at Crooked River and Haun's Mill.

I append the secret location of Shiloh Swales, below. Commit this location to memory and then destroy it.

[bottom edge of letter burned away]

———◆———

DUST TO DUST

[*Journal of Charles du Jeu, Friend and Partner to Dr. Beauregard "Buckshot" Cobb*]

[*first twenty-three pages illegible due to ruddy stain*]

04 Jan, 1858

[*illegible*] into camp at dusk and beg'd for scrapes [*scraps*] denied them. They drove oft our dogs then fell aground and gather'd bacon rines [*rinds*] and lick'd gravy from our pots. These poor Sius [*Sioux*] come on where we campt by a tree with a dead injin in its branches all rapt in a blanket and drest in red and raised to Heaven as is there custom, so sed [*said*] our Agent. 'Twas the first tree we seen in four days and we much remark'd on the dead injin in it. Dr. Cobb's Boy William is much thrill'd by every Kansas injin we seen as is his wife Sarah and their twin girls Emily and Ester. They are both of a size and are a curious set and ask of the Agent more questions about injins than in ten lifetimes I could think to ask. Emily hopes to please us each with her little gifts of one kind or a nother while Ester has eyes but for her Mother. Tho a Sin to put this fine family at risk on an adventure of this Kind, our disguise is a good one, and the Cobb girls has been plenty good company. I would stand for not a hair harm'd on the head of any a one of them and nor would the Doc. Thus they are in good hands with the Doc the fiercest fighter I ever know'd who aint never bled a drop. Our healths are comfortable our situation is fine and we have not yet seen nothing terrible. Come on twelve miles and campt at a small spring and here kill'd an antelope.

04 Jan, 1858

We come on at dawn and the Sius [*Sioux*] still a follow'd. Here past a ded injin raised up on a scaffold near to the Good Spirit as they could get him. Here bones of another scatter'd in a draw where this poor Creature got hack'd asunder by others of his Kind. The Sius stopt to pray and to build for him a scaffold to prop his bones and we seed no more of them. Stopt for the night along a creek with a clifft of rocks on the opesite side. Here kill'd an antelope.

10 Jan, 1858

[*illegible passage*] was so thirste [*thirsty*] he suckt mud to cool his swell'd tongue from days w/o water. The Idiot come on many miles to molest us for flour and sed [*said*] to Dr. Cobb what sort of doctor are you until our Agent was obliged to fall back. William taked his tobacco (2 lbs) and Dr. Cobb gived his knife to the Agent. It was a good knife of better Kind than ever I seen. Wether is mild.

12 Jan, 1858

Come on a cold morning w water froze in our pans. Here grass is chew'd so short the horses cant fix a bite. The Agent sed [*said*] here the grasshoppers fill the skies like a blizzerd and them hoppers is what done such Evil unto the grass. Here past a traders post where a white feller lived with his squaw who rest'd in the shade and knew no more of work than the dogs grubbing round her. Here they ask'd 20 dollars for a hundred weight of flour w beetles and Doc Cobb sed [said] he'd eat a buffalo chip afore he gived them a dime. Here no trees of any Kind. Here wind blous [blows] til you could stir it with a stick. Seen grave of a white Boy of aged 7, same as Emily. We remarkt on our good fortune and consider'd the misery apt suffer'd by the poor family who buried this child. Here was a solum [solemn] Night. Campt in the open country near Boy's grave and spoke fue. Bitter cold. Burn'd sage and cow chips to warm our dumplings. Here the Agent kill'd a kioti [coyote] and ate its tung [tongue]. Sposin this Savage would devour a dog if we allow'd it.

13 Jan, 1858

Come on thirty miles to the bottoms near Apache Rock. Trail soft and perilous. One pony ment for little Ester got bog'd so bad only her Hed was free. Could not free it kwick [quick] and It dyed. Poor girls much bereaved over the situation and wept much o'er the Beast. We at last pull'd it free and butcher'd It for a smoking. Here Sarah kill'd a fat kwail.

14 Jan, 1858

Laid up at Bottoms yet. Kill'd to fat kwails and a [unreadable word].

15 Jan, 1858

Laid up at Bottoms yet. Sent Agent a scouting for Apache Rock. Rest'd well and look'd at letters of B. Young and M. Goddard, a Crooked River Boy. Dr. Cobb recalls M. Goddard well enuf [enough] from our scrape

at Haun's Mill and Goddard's young wife Luretia who
got ravaged to days by them Miseri [Missouri] Devils
who taked her. Sposin that snakebit daughter Ada might
of even got sired by them rapests if rithmatic serves.
Ester remark'd on that big reward we was apt to collect
and at that the Dr. show'd her Ada's lock of yellow
hair and remarkt for an hour on the horror of Haun's
Mill and all them Mormons suffer'd. He remarkt to
them girls on that terrible seen [scene] that so changed
him for Ever that he went a warrin aside the Mormons
against them M Devils ever since and later again with J
Brown against the same evil sonsabitches. Sposin Doc
Cobb would travel most-way to Hell for the chance to
kill them sonsabiches some more and sposin I'd follow
him there for want of the verry same. Good company.
Got X.L.NT horse meat a plenty. Ester and Emily
played there games and collect'd there stones and shells
and seem'd not so bereaved o'er the death of there pony.
All in fair spirits. Girls make shell necklaces. Men talkt
night away. No where on Airth are finer Friends than
these.

16 Jan, 1858

Come on airly to Day for bitter winds blou'd from
the NE. Came on about 20 miles and campt in lee of
queer domed hill. Agent remarkt it was burial mound of
an older Kind of injin than now habits the Plains and
thus did not please Him and he would not come near it.
No wood anywhere. Burn'd sage and dry chips. Hear'd
geese all around but seen none. Strange Day. Windyest
Night ever Blou'd and cold as bones. We pray tomorrow
brings less deplorable wether.

17 Jan

Awoke to terrible [illegible] both girls is taked

18 Jan, 1858

No sign of girls horses and dogs. No sign of Agent. Sposin Agent taked and sold the lot of them him Self. Found where Kiowa train was campt in a swale (3 m. W) and seen there pole tracks drag'd into ground south bound'd. Will and Doc. go after Kiowas while I stay'd w Sarah. Is terrible situation She can not be console'd.

19 Jan, 1858

Laid up yet in lee of Mound. No sign of C or W or Ag. Verry cold. Burn'd chips to thaw horse meat but Sarah ate none of it. Slept none. Sarah weeps and sircles [circles] and holler'd all night for Girls and wont take no whiskey.

20 Jan, 1858

To Day return'd safe C and W but w/o Girls. Kiowas drived them oft afore they got close. Was out number'd. See'd no sign of Girls but find'd Agent ded and hack'd asunder on the Prarie [prairie] so he is forgivin any Sin. Train of light wagons came on at Dark and stopt and hear'd our tale and share'd there rabbets and dumplings. One woman from St. Joe among them had one week ago buried her ded Girl and she wept much w Sarah for all she suffer'd in her Kind. They give'd us a mule but no horses to spare. We must to

Morrow leave this terrible Place and move on w/o horses.

22 Jan, 1858

Come on 20 miles yester Day and 20 more to Day w/o no words spoken. Crosst to creeks and paid the same injin a nickel per head to ford them for no dout more injins was a wait'd near by. Campt in a low spot. No trees or wood. Boil'd beans o'er chips and sage. Two injins come in for Dinner. One leav'd and come back w 4 squaws and papooses and we give'd them beans to. One squaw clasp'd her hands and sed a prayer to the Good Spirit for the lost girls. Sarah to sick w despair to enjoy these kind Womens company.

24 Jan, 1858

Much snow and ice come upon us in the night and the mule is froze and dyed. Sarah has took verry sick and must be carried.

25 Jan, 1858

More snow upon us and trail is lost. All on foot now and Sarah has Xaust'd. None fit to carry her no further. Campt in lee of a short clifft where wind still blous fierce and could not raise no fire as all is wet'd and froze. To Night ate snow and froze horse meat. Meat gone now. Sarah has terrible sick and takes no Whiskey. Doc bled her and gived her bolts of lard and pepper in sted.

DUST TO DUST

26 Jan, 1858

Our deer Sarah is dyed.

27 Jan, 1858

Laid up yet account of Blizzerd.

30 Jan, 1858

Laid up yet. Blizzerd not abated. No fire five days nor food. Ground froze to hard to bury Sarah. Is deplorable situation.

03 Feb, 1858

Laid up yet. Starve'd haff [half] near ded. Talkt to Night about cure for situation. W study on this more. God forgive us whate'r we do.

05 Feb, 1858

Come on a Lone [alone] about five miles w new vigour. Blizzerd stopt but deep snow yet covers trail and I may be oft It. I have taked ill and worry'd if I should dye to in this froze place like Sarah. Campt in draw where was heap'd light wagons and hack'd corpses and I burn'd them all wood and bones and drinkt whiskey and ate meat from my sack and rais'd such a fire as could be seen from Heaven!

M. C. NORRIS

06 Feb, 1858

Sposin I seen smoke and push hard toward place I seen it. Hope yet to find lost Girls. Must be close to Cimarron R. Only Dr. knows. Doc gone. Campt a Lone in a sandy situation and drank Whiskey and rais'd big fire and ate much meat and here sposin I hear'd Sarah a hollerin thru the night but It was only wind in the Dark. Got lost my camp and fire gone. Have but meat and pistol terrible Night!

07 Feb, 1858

Come on a Lone to sandy situation here found Mens tracks in a draw and follow'd them round til trail stopt in bad snow where is burn'd wagons and corpses in blizzerd and I kill'd a wild Dog and rais'd Fire from coals! Campt a Lone in this queer place til Doc C and William catch'd Me at Dark and was verry angery w/ Me -- remarkt here we stay to Gether for Ever! Shoot oft no more guns at Dogs and should have rais'd no big fires like I done. W taked my Whiskey and throw'd my sack of meat and I sed to Him sposin I go a scouting again to Morrow for place I seen smoke and find Sarah/Kiowas and let all wild Dogs a Lone and W sed sposin I in sted go to Hell! Doc and W verry unhappy w me but say not why. Tho blizzerd w Dogs yet terrible can not abate.

[end of journal by Charles du Jeu]

DUST TO DUST

[from the physician's journal of Dr. Beauregard "Buck-shot" Cobb]

19 February, 1858
Physician's Journal

A Description of Shiloh Swales.

The lost colony of Shiloh Swales is but a queer collection of domed hills situated a few leagues from the southern woods rimming the lowlands that shed down into the Cimarron River valley. The settlement is beset on all sides by untended fields that race for leagues in every direction. Defensive bunkers at each of the four cardinal points. Approximately twenty domed hills of about the size of an ordinary railcar, all staved in on their south facing slopes with dugouts, crudely excavated, where Mormons once must have thrived like a colony of termites. Have heard no more of that terrible shrieking that led William and I all through the night to this place. No sign of anyone here but a pair of wild young boys who have spent the whole morning ducking through the ghostly commons. Shall fire a warning shot at noon, then engage them.

[From the Diary of Early Goddard]

19 February, 1858

Round noon today a pair of men aint never before beheld fired a shot and walked right into Shiloh Swales through the middle of the third field. I never knew a

70

rougher looking sight as these two, all starved and frost bit and confused. Little Enis was ready to shoot the both of them in the field but Papa warned him back, then started for them as tho he'd a knowed them all his life. I never seen Papa so bothered by anything. How Papa can know a fellow from outside Shiloh Swales is beyond me, but I now reckon he might once have travelled farther than we now are able, Indians being so troublesome.

Mam set about a cleaning and a cooking beans, but Papa said they was not yet fit for company and first needed a heap of rest. He said no more than that these men had suffered hard to find us in the wilderness, and we boys would earn a whipping if we bothered them or wandered near their door. Papa put them both up in Hiram Merrick's old dugout.

19 February, 1858

Papa has returned from H. Merrick's quarters and now speaks alone with Mam on his learnings of the strange new men. Enis and I was sent outside the dugout and told not to pry, but who could help but pry a little. The new men was sent to us as part of a rescue party. They hail from a place to the east called Lawrence, and they buried five along the trail. One fellow among their lost went lunatick in a blizzard and was killed by his companions for terrible acts. This is all we learned of them. Now I fear for poor Ada, that these men will not tolerate her condition. I pray for the sun to shine on whatever day these men are fit to pay a visit, such that Ada will keep still.

20 February, 1858

Still the strangers rest. Will they ever wake? Little Enis wants so bad to steal a look at them that he is bound to earn the both of us a whipping. Ada has been peaceful all day after an awful spell, last night. Mam keeps the curtain drawn round her bed. Next month will make a year since she got snakebit. Mam asked Enis and I to catch and pick all the geese right after thaw. Reckon she aims to make a feather bed. I pray she don't intend the new bed for these two men, or I'd suppose they plan to stay a long while. I fear they will sooner than not discover Ada, if she suffers another spell as terrible as the last.

21 February, 1858

The new men have come to stir a bit for the first time in two days. Never seen men so tired as these. Papa says they may be fit for a visit by tomorrow eve. I asked if they might noon with us instead, and Papa said not to worry, as Ada was in no danger from these men, who mostly come here on account of her. One of them is a Doctor sent to cure her. The other is the Doctor's son. I wonder what sort of Doctor would kill one of his own party for misbehaviour? How that does affright me! I forever wonder what terrible sin the lunatick committed to earn his killing. Last night brought another bad spell. Seems as though Ada senses the visitors and aims to make herself known to them. The new blood does inspire great curiosity in all of us, as we've had no Others in Shiloh Swales for almost one year.

M. C. NORRIS

22 February, 1858

The new men are mostly recovered and are now about. They are not yet moved from the old Merrick dugout, but they sun themselves on the stoop like a pair of lizards, smoking their pipes in their underwear. They are as filthy a set as I've ever beheld, in terrible need of bath and shear. The elder is named Dr. Beauregard "Buckshot" Cobb, and his grown son is named William. They introduced themselves to Enis and I, and they seem pleasant enough. They speak a lot of the other folks whom they buried along the way, as I suppose is a natural thing. Two of those five lost were a couple of girls, aged nigh the same as Enis and I. Thus, we was very disappointed to hear such bad news, as we've had no other children in Shiloh Swales for a long while, and never no girls aged same as we. Josiah Campbell was our last good friend, and we still miss him terribly and speak of him often. How merry it might have been if God had spared those two girls. We pray the Consumption don't take our guests too soon.

Dr. Cobb intends to examine Ada this afternoon. And for this evening, Mam invited our new friends to supper. Mam has promised a king's feast of roast goose, pickled tumbleweeds and taters!

———◆———

[from the physician's journal of Dr. Beauregard "Buckshot" Cobb]

22 February, 1858
Phsycian's Journal

The Examination of Ada Goddard.

The terrible stench was first to greet me, as I stooped to clear the Goddard's low threshold. 'Twas dark and very cold inside their dugout, due to the northerly orientation of their doorway ('tis perhaps worthy of note that the Goddard's dugout is unique to all the rest, in this respect). Due to hardship, I presume, no fire burned in their hearth, and not a single candle was lit. Here hung the cloying stench of aged and ample decomposition permitted to dampen in the wet seasons and desiccate again in the dry. Here was the stench of an open grave. And when my eyes at last accustomed to the gloom, I beheld the source of it, upon a featherbed.

Collapsed flesh the colour of gypsum terminated in yellowed claws that curled inward to her wrists, and a head crooked back over a stained pillow with lips stretched round in a silent howl. By God, were it not for the chill of winter solstice, she would be a blackened husk, roiling with maggots.

"Shame on all of you!" said I. "Shame on all of you for inviting a Doctor here!" For this girl Ada was dead by many months. They begged me that I should stay with them longer, but of late I've beheld enough of death and winter madness and the like that I would willingly tolerate no more of either.

Very upset. I intend for William and I to quit this place and return for Lawrence just as soon as weather permits.

M. C. NORRIS

[From the Diary of Early Goddard]

22 February, 1858

    I knew it was a mistake to let the new men see Ada, so soon. I knew they would be unhappy by the sight of her, and now they wish to leave us. Would only they come to know her like we do. Would only they stay a while longer and see Ada after dark, up to her regular tricks.

⸺◈⸺

[from the physician's journal of Dr. Beauregard "Buck-shot" Cobb]

22 February, 1858
Phsycian's Journal

The Kindly Persuasion of Enis Goddard.

    After noon, the youngest Goddard boy, little Enis, risked a whipping to pay William and I a visit. He did implore me with fanatical conviction to return with him to his family dugout at evefall, for at that time I would behold some great and terrible change that occurs nightly to the remains of his sister. Against my better judgment, I did agree that if it should so please him, William and I would still attend the supper that his poor Mother had already commenced to prepare--provided the meal was to be served here, of course, and not in the company of the corpse--and later take a second look at Ada. To this offer, young Enis and his elder brother showed profound enthusiasm.

The boys are a wild set, barely civilized and wholly inseparable after so long a time spent alone together in this wilderness that they call home. Though the elder boy, Early, appears somewhat wan and sickly, he remains yet spry enough to keep pace with little Enis as they dart through their abandoned colony like rabbits through a warren. I say, these lads do remind me of old Charles and I, back in our younger years, the way they chase and tease. I do miss Charles terribly, and my regret over this adventure is a guilt beyond measure.

[From the Diary of Early Goddard]

22 February, 1858

We have at last spent an eve with our new friends, Dr. Cobb and William, and enjoyed our King's feast in the old dugout of Hiram Merrick. It was a pleasure to sup there with them, and to remember the good meals we once enjoyed there, in the company of Brother Merrick and his family. The new men look a heap different and better after a hot bath and grooming. Mam rooted through plenty of empty dugouts to find new clothes to best suit each of them. The adults sent Enis and I to bed while they sit a while, and the new men smoke their pipes. Dr. Cobb has promised to return here after nightfall and examine Ada a second time. No longer do I fear the good Doctor, for he is a kind and brilliant man who presents to us no danger. Papa told Enis and I that the Doctor is also a very brave man, who has shed much blood in sympathy for noble causes. His grown son William is a quieter sort with a gentle habit of ducking his eyes from Mam and we children.

M. C. NORRIS

———•+•—•—•—•+•—•———

[from the physician's journal of Dr. Beauregard "Buckshot" Cobb]

23 February, 1858
Physician's Journal

The Curious Case of Ada Goddard.

'Twas after supper while William and I smoked
our pipes and conversed with Marshall and Luretia
Goddard that our host was stilled midsentence by a
shriek so colossal that William and I nigh came off our
seats with fright. It came from the direction of the
Goddard dugout. The Goddards then said to us that Ada
had awoken, and asked us if we were prepared to come
and see her. Though the Goddards appeared earnest, my
William and I did look at once to one another with the
same terrible suspicion that this was perhaps a deadly
trick designed to deprive us both of our lives. And when
the shriek came a second time, our pistols fast emerged
from our belts. Luretia begged we leave our pistols
behind lest we shoot Ada upon sight, and I replied that
we most certainly would not do either. She then insisted
we leave our candles as Ada's eyes were sensitive to
light, and that the moonlight should suffice. To that
request I assured the woman that a candle was positively
needed for a proper examination, but that it would be
held as far from her daughter's eyes as possible.

As we forded the darkness between the Goddard's
dugout and our own, the shrieks and the growls seemed
to become ever more fearsome. Our doorways face one
another from a distance of eighty feet, so the path we

traveled was relatively straight and clear but for an emergent stone or two. Hands upon shoulders we followed the flickering candle held by Marshall Goddard, who led us through the night. Marshall cupped his hand before the flame in an effort to appease the upset Thing, for its braying became frantic as candlelight spilled over the Goddards' doorway. Marshall knocked, as though the dwelling were not his own. Momentarily, the elder boy answered, and admitted we four into the lightless room.

Prepared though I was for the same intolerable stench, the odor of this afternoon had wholly dissipated. In its place was a not unpleasant medley of sulfur and sweet milk. The room's temperature, it seemed, had been raised without fire to a warmth greater than it ought be, such that I began to perspire.

There she lay, wholly unclothed upon the featherbed as before, yet every aspect of Ada Goddard had changed. Rotund and full breasted as though she was with child, she had been tethered, wrists and ankles, to the steel frame of her bed. I did not observe that she breathed with any regularity, but one breath sharply drawn did precede her every purr and growl. I placed my fingertips upon her forearm and she began to writhe. Cold as January snow, her skin, and if her heart did beat at all, its pulse was so weak that I could not detect it. I then asked her Mother how often does she eat and drink and evacuate her bowels, and to this question Luretia looked fearfully to Marshall as though I'd stumbled nigh the precipice of some imminent scandal. After an awkward moment, Luretia then assured me that Ada did perform every natural function, from time to time.

Ada's face was so covered by that mat of yellow hair that it afforded an illusion that her head was twisted owlishly round. Trading my pistol to Marshall for the candle he kept, I lowered the flame nigh her face, where yellow hair rose and fell with every rasp. I parted the dank curtain to reveal rosebud lips. So taut and desiccated by Day, they were now pouty with renewed youth and bejeweled with perspiration. Further, I explored, following the curve of a nostril up the bridge of her nose until a dilated pupil receded into its amber pool. An inhuman growl resounded from deep within her throat, and I drew my hand away as her pretty mouth then gaped like a serpent poised to swallow a hen's egg. She flexed and contracted her jaw to the point that it seemed to dislocate, and her chin hung full upon her throat in a toothless horror. I then recoiled, as from the roof of Ada's mouth dropped a set of hooked fangs that stretched tight against their sheaths like the leather sacking of a drawn bellows. Her eye flicked my way. As she fixed her glare upon me, twin jerks of yellowish fluid sprayed from those wicked points, arching over her bare breasts to her loins. Clasping hands with Luretia Goddard, I then fell upon my knees and joined the Goddards in a prayer vigil that lasted through the night. Peace at last arrested the girl's twisted countenance at dawn's first light, when she died again for the hundredth time as winter birds began to twitter.

PART FOUR OF SIX:

SAVAGE DOCTOR, BRILLIANT BEAST

The boy lowered the journal into his lap. Sitting Indian-style on the dusty floorboards, he closed his eyes and extended himself, through his sense of hearing, to a range beyond the clapboard walls. Thin moments drifted by until his whole body jerked when he heard it again, the same sound of fluttering wings.

His eyes flicked open, blinked. He placed the journal on the floor and hitched himself to his feet, cocking one ear to skyward to the schoolhouse ceiling. There—something was scratching at the roof. The boy edged away from the sprung cedar chest, and he backed toward a boarded window where moonlight reamed through every chink. His heart hammering, he rotated toward the portal, bulged eyes nearing those knotty slats. Some part of him half-expected to see Dracula himself reared and hissing in the schoolyard, like he posed in that poster hanging over in

Liberal's theater that had been scaring kids off the sidewalk since '31. He peered through the slats. Thank heavens, there were no Draculas outside.

The schoolyard stretched bright and clear as a moonlit snowfield, bone-white and awhirl with a tumult of shadows. They were dizzying to look upon, the way they swirled and reveled over the grass like tiny fragments of the night ripped loose from their place in the heavens and given leave. The dark shards chittered and scooped low through the earth's wavering heat before hurtling back into the safety of the skies.

Bats. That's all they were. The boy curled his fingertips through the slats and closed his eyes, breathing deeply, silently thanking the good Lord for sparing him the sight of something worse. But even with his eyes clamped shut, his imagination continued to project the flickering image of Bela Lugosi on the twin screens that were the backsides of his eyelids, where the monster's claws gripped that damsel's pale throat ... *A Nightmare of Horror!*

He'd never actually seen the film. But he wasn't blind to those glaring similarities between that Dracula on the poster and someone else the boy had once known. But then, there were some pretty obvious differences, too. That glossy cape, made-up face and severely slickered hair made Bela Lugosi look more like a Kansas City dandy than anyone distantly related to that scalded monster in the storm. Enis sure had himself a set of fangs, and then he'd died just the way a Dracula was supposed to die when he got a wooden stake jammed through his thumper—that was supposed to be the surest way to kill them. But whether it was the Comanche arrow that had done Enis in, or the lightning strike that sent him up in flames like a pile of old tires, the boy couldn't be sure.

Looking back, the boy recalled that Enis did like to smoke those old cigars, and he sure handled his matches without much worry. But when you considered the moonshine explosion that melted his face like a dollop of butter, and the lightning strike that reduced him to a pile of greenish ash, it would seem as though Draculas were a darned sight more combustible than all the hocus pocus let on. Goddard had gone up in flames so fast, it was as if he'd had pure lantern fuel running through his veins. He'd sure tended to avoid the sun, moving only by night, or under the cover of black dusters. Maybe all the comics and pulp books he'd studied over the years only had it about half-right. It was from those poor resources that he'd form-ulated his theories, because they were all he'd had to study, until now.

The boy flinched at the muffled thump of a small body on the schoolhouse roof. He could hear tiny claws scratching against the tarpaper as it dragged itself toward the peak. Another one bumped into the east wall. Outside, their cachinnating trills resonated through the starlit sky.

The boy heeled away from the boarded window. Had to get finished up with his reading before daybreak, when Mildred and Levin Byers would show up to start banging around inside their creamery. Lots of unanswered ques-tions remained. Besides needing answers, he still hadn't gotten past that niggling feeling that despite having sur-vived his tooth-and-nail showdown against the Devil himself, he might've only just scratched the surface of Eden's darkest secret. The idea of cowering in the shadow of some phantom threat was not a condition by which the boy cared to live out the remainder of his days. Wasn't in his nature. His Mam had taught him that it was best to face your problems head-on than to slink around them like a stray dog. She'd always said, "It feels a darned sight better to wash your hands of dirty business than to go off to bed feeling filthy."

Pap, on the other hand, was a different sort of animal than his Mam had ever been. He was a tough old passive, every bit as hardworking and stubborn as those mules he loved to hate, while Mam engaged life like a bull. Pap had one hellbender of a temper, but rarely did he ever direct the brunt of it onto anyone or anything beyond some inanimate object, like a tangled coil of rope or a bolt with a stripped-off head. But for the most part, he was the quiet one who kept his head down and his mind focused on the job at hand, letting life's bullets just bounce right off him rather than ever returning fire. The boy liked to believe that was because Pap was probably packing an elephant gun, and knew it, so the crack of small arms fire didn't rile him. He always seemed to have an agenda that he never shared, expecting you to jump whenever he said so. He didn't like answering questions. You had to pester the hell out of him for a half-answer, if you were lucky. Of the two, Pap was by the more frustrating, the more difficult to appreciate and understand. Mam, on the other hand, kept nothing hidden behind her back. She carried it all right up front for the world to see. Bright as a sparkler, she'd light up a room, and her laugh, God bless... you could've heard that cackle in the next county. The boy caught himself smiling in the dusty gloom.

The smile faded when he thought of the mean switch that Pap was bound to put to his ass if he learned he'd broken into the old schoolhouse a second time. But this time, it wasn't Comanche souvenirs that he was after. These were far more serious times. What he sought was closure on the mystery of Enis Goddard, and at the risk of Pap's switch, he hoped tonight he'd finally put to rest his worst fear of all—that there could be more than one of them.

---

24 February, 1858
Physician's Journal

The Mythology of the Old World Revenant, and the New World Consumptive.

Two days I have spent in the deepest consideration of all that I have witnessed, hereto. Twice more by day, I have examined the sad corpse of Ada Goddard, and all through the night of the 23rd, I endured her regular screams. Over the course of my own life, I have heard every diverse sound of human suffering, both in the hospital and on the battlefield, but never have I heard such beastly ululations of this kind. Though I assured the Goddards that I would still seek to find a cure for their ailing daughter, I would rather face the whole of the Missouri Militia than to ever again spend a night in the Goddard dugout.

The curious case of Ada Goddard aside, there are yet many mysteries here in Shiloh Swales, of which the Goddards seem reluctant to speak. With the exception of the Goddard family, no Others have been spared in what was once a thriving colony. Where have they all gone? While Marshall Goddard has implied that these erstwhile tenants died mostly within the last year, he appears reluctant to divulge any detail on the apparent plague that consumed them. Nor have I, in my daily explorations of this place, encountered a single grave. If the Mormons did die, then where are they buried? Out of respect to my kind hosts and all they must have suffered, I have not yet made demands for a detailed explanation. For the present, I intend to focus my every faculty on the task of curing Ada Goddard of the Evil that has fastened itself to her.

I am no great doctor or scholar, but I have found that in this world there are Evils of body and mind that remain apart from the scope of science in their resistance to diagnosis and to method of treatment. Whatever it is that appears intent on molesting this girl and her family is no malady known to me, nor one described in any respectable journal of medicine.

'Twas a belief long held by our elder Physicians and Holymen that diverse Faeries, Daemons and Spirits were responsible for incurable Evils. Thus, in many instances in our common past, great hardships and other anfractuosities were oft been blamed upon these sorts of creatures that fastened themselves to fools trespassing through places known and shunned for ages. Perhaps the worst of these entities is a Daemon Spirit of the Old World oft described by those woeful English Custodians who dug so many thousands of graves during the Black Plague. This Daemon was believed to take possession of the newly buried Dead. And the name they gave to this hated Thing was The Revenant.

The Revenant was believed to habit lightless places like dank caverns, wells and most especially human graves, where it bothered the corpses, therein. The Dead awakened by the magick of this Spirit were but husks wherein the Revenant dwelled, and by the light of day, maintained every likeness, thereof. But after Evefall, those corpses stirred by their Master's hand were made to quit their graves and feed like leeches upon the living.

A comparison, here, is perhaps worthy of reference, between the lore of the Old World Revenant and the New World Consumptive, for their distinct similarities may perhaps provide a new perspective on the curious case of Ada Goddard.

Though the ordinary malady of Consumption is a disorder of the lungs, there have been peculiar cases that more closely afflict the heart, which have yielded corpses resistant to decay. 'Tis these curious cases that have inspired the quiet conclusion amongst Physicians and Scholars that this latter form of Consumption may not be a disease of the body at all, but the effect of spiritual visitation by the dead Consumptive upon the Living. So long as the exhumed corpse of a dead Consumptive has red blood inside its body, it has been deemed proof, by those presiding, that an occult influence is stealing blood from the Living without ever breaking the skin. This black magick ultimately brings about the death and spiritual possession of the victims, after a marked and suffering decline.

Consider the Ray Family of Connecticut, 1854: a Father and two Sons all three died of Consumption, and a fourth relative had taken ill. In an effort to spare the life of this relative, the Ray Family exhumed all the bodies of the dead Consumptives, cut out their hearts, and burned them. At least one of these corpses was reported to have been bloated and smug in appearance, *its mouth slathered with the same blood that filled its heart and stomach.*

Reports of this kind are not numerous, but in every case, 'tis a situation of close proximity between the Living and the Dead that seems to attract the so-called Revenant Spirit. Likewise, in every case where the Revenant was thwarted, the relatives did exhume the corpses of dead Consumptives and removed their heads and/or vital organs and destroyed them with fire. It could therefore be supposed that the lifelike condition of a dead Consumptive and physical possession by the Revenant Spirit are one in the same condition, all caused by Living Blood in close proximity to the Evil's place of rest.

In the first leg of our journey, we did observe the common practice of the Indians to elevate Corpses high above the Airth in the branches of trees or upon scaffolds. By contrast, the ordinary practice of the ancient Indians was to heap great mounds or hills of airth and to bury their Dead, therein. For reasons unknown to me, that old prac-tice has been wholly abandoned by the Redskinned Kind and these old burial mounds are shunned and despised. Thus, I deduce the reason the Savages come not within a league of Shiloh Swales may in fact be because every dwelling in this damned colony was carelessly situated into the slopes of ancient burial mounds. The Mormons' intrusion into this holy place is most surely a capital offense, hence, the Savages fall upon them like lions the instant they quit their unwholesome sanctuaries and start for the fields. For this sin, I can not judge them, but perhaps God and the Indians already have.

By day, Ada Goddard slumbers the sleep of the Dead. But a shift from sloth to wakefulness occurs

Nightly, and on any Day when clouds or dust storms blot out the Sun. Light of any kind She finds intolerable. To accommodate their daughter's queer condition, the Goddards have excavated a North facing dugout that keeps cold and dark to Ada's liking. By day, they keep a curtain drawn tightly around her, so no ray of sunlight is permitted to touch her skin.

I fear that there is little doubt that this Creature would destroy the Goddard family if they permitted for one instant her bonds to be loosened. I call her a Creature because I have come to the conclusion that the human spirit of Ada Goddard did naturally pass away, one year ago, due to the bite of a common rattlesnake. The nature of the life essence that fills her now, I do submit at the risk of my professional reputation, is no more human than that of the serpent that did her in.

With respect to a cure, I intend tomorrow to seek out the Savages and make peace with them. I must earn the favor of a local Healer if there is any hope in curing Ada, for the task at hand is beyond my own capacity.

God be with me, when I first encounter them.

25 February, 1858
Physician's Journal

William has left me, this morning, while I slept. It would appear that he stole a peek at my last journal entry, for he expressed in his parting letter his aim to spare me further peril by seeking out the Savages, him Self.

God bless my poor William who has lost so much on this terrible journey. Yet he is now so focused on saving the Goddards from their plight. Perhaps he aims to succeed with this family where we failed so miserably to spare his own. Though we have spoken some of the Girls, of poor Charles, and even of the Agent, dear Sarah's name has not been uttered since the day we buried what remained of her. What a terrible adventure this has been. Can we ever find happiness again? God willing, I pray that William shall, for neither one of us can bear the thought of any harm coming to the other. God spare him as he walks amongst the Savages. There is no Man on Airth I trust more than my son. He has the Hunter's spirit in his blood.

26 February, 1858
Physician's Journal

Nooned with the Goddards and discussed our future plans. Since the Mountain Meadows Massacre of last year, every trail is much imperiled with men eager for Mormon scalps. There fore, I implored they abandon any evidence of their Religion when they return back East with me to Lawrence, where the Free Staters will afford them sanctuary until 'tis safe for them to join a Westbound wagon train to Utah. The Goddards follow my reasoning, but the thought of destroying their sacred books and artifacts and all outward evidence of their Religion brings to them terrible duress, as their Faith is the central pillar of their lives and I believe they would prefer martyrdom over cowardice. They must study upon this for a spell while I continue to attend to Ada.

'Twould be difficult for anyone to harshly judge this family, despite their rather macabre eccentricities. Mrs. Luretia Goddard is a fine cook and a remarkable woman. She and Marshall suffered unmentionable

brutality at the hands of the Missouri Militia at Haun's Mill. Marshall's face is webbed with scars from their corn knives and forever this man shall limp, as they shot out the caps of his knees. I remember well his injuries, having doctored him my Self. Their two boys are a devoted pair of sons. The affect on either one of them would be grave, should any terrible misfortune befall the Other. To this bond between them I sympathize, as I lost dear Charles, who was in every aspect but blood my younger brother. Thus, I am inspired to look past their peculiarities and fulfill my promise to deliver this family from that Thing in their midst that seems so intent on destroying them. Clearly, Ada's effect is markedly worse upon Luretia and Early than upon Marshall and Enis. Precisely why the former are more sensitive to her Evil I have yet to determine.

27 February, 1858
Physician's Journal

Awoke this morning to the sound of shots fired, then the voice of Marshall Goddard in my doorway, rousting me with news of Indians. From the bunker on the south point, he spotted four Indians at daybreak slipping along the back edge of their field, and he discharged every weapon at hand until they were out of sight. For this warlike course of action, I did chastise him, as the Indians had not yet done us any wrong and he has thus imperiled our situation, and most particularly the situation of my son, who may be amongst them. I inquired as to the Indians' appearance being in any way related to William's departure, but with respect to this coincidence, Marshall was uncertain. I pray that no harm has come to my son. Very upset with Marshall Goddard for his profound ignorance.

Marshall intends to remain on point in the southern bunker all this day with Enis, and perhaps the next, in case the Indians plan to attack. He has invited me to join he and Enis tonight on their regular watch, while Early shall remain in the dugout, as always, to guard Luretia and Ada.

Early and Lurie (as he calls his wife), have struggled with their poor healths for a long spell, but in recent days have fallen more ill than ever. Regrettably, I must enter that unwholesome cave of theirs and tend to them. Mormon law forbids the drink of Whiskey, so I will prescribe to them a bloodletting, a dose of mercury, and regular bolts of lard and pepper.

28 February, 1858
Physician's Journal

The night in the bunker passed without noteworthy event. No hostility yet from the Indians, though we have heard the foreboding cadence of their war drums. A pack of coyotes to the east got wound to a fuss. 'Twas torturous to hear the beckoning howls from wilder and better lands than this one. Here, no joy nor pleasure comes to an old Hunter from the daily life. How the Goddards have tolerated this depraved existence for so long is perhaps the greatest mystery of all, in Shiloh Swales. Still very upset with M. Goddard over our situation, which has immeasurably worsened, as we cannot easily escape. My loyalty to this mission has yet been for naught, and I now so lament the haste with which I foolishly agreed to this adventure without careful consideration of the stakes. For the Goddards, I have lost nigh everything, and they do not seem appreciative in the least. Tonight, I drink, and leave the Goddards to their watch, for 'twas they who created this damnable situation.

I recall a time when William's mother once chastised me with regularity for my affection for bloody peril. She thought the wilderness a terrible place, a primordial arcade of chaos peopled by troglodytes that ought be well beneath a man of my education. And O, how she loathed the common company I cared to keep, like dear Charles, who was admittedly lacking in the refined manner she so highly appraised. Salt of the Airth, she called he and his kind. But in her eyes I was perhaps the greater fool for failing to rise above his kind and achieve affluence. But a predilection of that sort is simply not in the nature of the beast that I am, always have been, and always shall be.

What William's mother failed to see was that dear Charles and I were not different creatures at all, but one in the same beast, bound to the same charter. Although I was blessed, or perhaps cursed, with a greater capacity than he, in the sense that I was able to see to distances beyond his natural limitations, a beast endowed with greater faculties than his brethren is no less a beast than they. Dear Charles and I appreciated in equal measure the same passion for those wild places and all the bloody chaos, therein, and 'tis a man's passion that chiefly defines him, assigning his charter amongst the ranks of Men. For 'tis my own observation that to one of four charters does every man belong: Warrior, Tradesman, Artist, or Hunter. Through the course of his life a man's passions may shift and wax and wane, but at his very core he is devoted to and defined by one, and 'tis that one passion to which he shall give his life.

The loneliest of the four charters is the Hunter, for 'tis the shunned wilderness that he calls his home. And how alone I've often felt there, even at Charles's side, for though we walked together as two Hunters through the Hunter's world, I was wholly unlike the rest of that world's inhabitants. I was a fly in the ointment: forever misunderstood and despised by wives; a disappointment and a troglodyte in the halls of educated and brilliant men; a respected anomaly within the ranks of my common kind; hailed savior and healer of the ailing; a tool, used and employed in the agendas of great leaders of Men, oft at the expense of any fool unlucky enough to have loved me, or to have ridden at my side. My God, I am my family's destroyer, the savage doctor. I am forever cursed to be the brilliant beast.

02 March, 1858
Physician's Journal

Still no word from William. My health is poor today, after a night of indulgence in whiskey. Thus, today the Goddards and I have kept apart, some. A cold snap is settling in, and the skies are racing. Ada's cries mingle with the prairie wind when clouds overcast the sun, and she is becalmed again when they break. I fear that a prolonged spell of inclement weather may bring about such mania as to exhaust Luretia to her end, and to drive the rest of us, perhaps, to the brink of madness. Marshall and Enis keep distanced from Ada's commotion. They remain at all hours in the bunker. I would join them, but in my pathetic condition I have resigned my Self to bed. When the sun breaks through the clouds, my eyes widen before the burning seam around the door frame, and moments later my eyelids fall as the sun slips back behind the front and the cries of Ada Goddard resume. I have come to find her guttural lows of yearning to be most intolerable. I am certain there are men in this world who might find her moans arousing, until a glimpse of that monster was thrust upon their eyes.

Sickly as she be, Lurie paid a visit this afternoon to deliver me jars of potted meat, potatoes and pickled stems of the tumbling weeds. I was shocked by her appearance, which has deteriorated to a ghastly pallor. She too reckons that a blizzard is rolling in, and we may be laid up for a week or more. There is not a stick of wood within a league of this wretched place. Thus, we must risk our lives to forage for buffalo chips in the fields before the storm is upon us.

I have discovered that William had the foresight to take with him one copy of the **Lecompton Constitution**, which might serve to save his life should he encounter that rumored Assembly of Missouri Squatters. Against the Savages, however, he has but his wits and his rifle. I beg the Lord for his safe return. My son is all that I have left in this world.

03 March, 1858
Physician's Journal

The blizzard is at last upon us. Still no sign of my son. It pains me to think of him out in the open country against this devilish weather. He is a strong young man with a keen knack for survival, but this country is not his own. I dare not dwell too long in such fatalism, lest

I join dear Charles in the winter madness that wholly consumed him.

The pickled weeds are tough and sinewy and sour as the vinegar brine. How the Goddards have survived so long on this wretched food is beyond me. The potted meat is not entirely of poor taste, but 'tis yet disagreeable to me, as my mouth is confused by its queer shapes and stringy texture. From what Airthly beast could this meat have been butchered? Perhaps 'tis that I cannot scour from my own mind the terrible events of our journey here, that now make meat of every kind seem unwholesome, darkly suspect. Tho William and I believed ourselves spared the terrible glamour that settled o'er poor dear Charles, I have come to fear that perhaps his quicker penance was more merciful than the deepening melancholy that threatens to consume my spirit. In this old Hunter's life, I've perhaps beheld too much, spent too much time in lonely places, for there no stain is more lasting than that of blood.

Through the blizzard, Ada serenades me Night and Day without relent. I watch over the Goddard dugout through my latch hole. I wait for a body to pass before their candles, as some reassurance that someone besides that shackled Daemon is yet spared. Each day brings me closer to the resolution that there can be no cure for Ada but by the burning of her Evil heart. Only this can save the Goddard family, if it pleases their God they be saved at all.

04 March, 1858
Physician's Journal

Eight days with no word from Charles. The blizzard has not let up for one instant. Outside, snow deepens with every passing minute. I know now what it is to be like Ada, the Living Dead, condemned to forever watch a bleak and ephemeral world slide past a knothole in one's coffin. It screams, It screams and It screams. Would only her featherbed be in line with my rifle's sights, I would end this.

Sundown—the day is done and Its shrieks have become regular as my own drawn breaths. I counted, over just the last hour, three-hundred and forty-four. 'Tis as though It puts forth a stupendous effort to ensure that each hour of my suffering is made more intolerable than the last. Every minute, that voice grows higher pitched and more piercing to the ears. 'Tis my blood for which this Thing yearns--of this I am certain--for this Thing has crawled up from Hell to take me, and here on this dead Mormon's bed It shall find me, pistol and Bowie crossed o'er my heart. Come for me, Ada, for I have naught to show God in my life's sad balance but the memories of my every beastly deed and the ghosts of my loved ones' every terrible end. O, but I have something that it would please me to show you, you screaming Banshee! My God, I know not how much more of this torture I ca— [badly stained, illegible]

[from the journal of Early Goddard]

04 March, 1858

Four shots fired in the night. There has been a fight of some kind, but Mam is so ill now that I would not leave her alone in her weakened state with Ada. On account of the storm, Ada is almost always awake and making a fuss. She never for an instant takes her eyes off poor Mam, who lies so still beside her, and looks so deathly wan, that I must make regular checks of her breath. I am trapped in the dugout, close enough to hear their shooting, but too far to halloo. I suppose I am lucky enough to have Ada for company, but I do miss Enis, out there with Papa in the blizzard. Surely the Indians would not scalp a little boy. That is my greatest fear of all. If Enis dies in any mean way, by God, I will turn Ada loose upon them. We know what Ada can do.

05 March, 1858

In the night Mam has lost her resolve to fight. Mam sleeps with Ada now. Our beloved Mam is gone.

05 March, 1858

I delivered news of Mam's passing to Papa and Enis, in the bunker. Praise God, for they are both still alive. Enis wept at the bad news and wondered why Mam gave in. Papa told him she could not stand to hear Ada cry no more.

Dr. Cobb is gone. Papa said he passed by the bunker in the night with his every weapon charged and shouldered and his mind was set on finding his missing son. He was so upset that he did not even stop to bid Papa farewell. Papa reckons his son William has got captured by the Indians, and that is why they are suddenly so brave. With all the Indians afoot, Dr. Cobb is by now dead or captured, himself. Dr. Cobb and William were sent to rescue us, but they have only delivered us greater misfortune, and finally, they have

*abandoned us. The Indians no doubt have an attack in
store. We three must soon leave here for the place called
Lawrence, after we take poor Mam and Ada to the
Comanche Vent, and send them down to God.*

[from the journal of Early Goddard]

07 March, 1858

*More fighting has erupted over the last two days
than ever before, so there has been no safe time to quit
this place. The Indians howl like demons, all around us,
and twice have they tried to set the fields afire, but the
fields are too wet to take. Two days and no word from
Papa or Enis, but I hear their shots fired every hour and
I pray many Indians they have killed.*

*Mam has begun to cry out like Ada. Mam and Ada
now look so much alike that I can hardly tell one from
the other.*

[from the journal of Early Goddard]

07 March, 1858

*Enis has returned! He came to see Mam for a short
while. He says he and Papa have killed a few, but the
pounding drums and howling from beyond the fields
means an attack is sure to come. Storm is worse than
ever. Mam and Ada can not rest. I told Enis of my idea
to turn them loose upon the Indians. But Enis loves
them, and he can not stand to let them go. He is too
young to understand.*

M. C. NORRIS

[from the journal of Early Goddard]

08 March, 1858

    I feel better and stronger today. Mam and Ada are at rest, for the storm has broke and today the sun shines and stills them. I am certain we must today take them to the Comanche Vent while they are quiet, so that we may slip past the Indians. I am not yet fit to load them into the wagon by myself, but at the risk of a whipping, I have wrapped them in quilts and dragged them both outside, forty yards from the dugout. I then set about to cleaning, turned the soiled featherbed, and started the first fire that this sad hearth has ever known. Now our dugout is warm and bright and cheerful, at last. If only Enis and Papa were here to enjoy this comfort with me. I hope they smell the smoke and return to noon with me. Two shots fired from the bunker, around sunrise. I pray our Indian war may soon abate. This morning's efforts have tired me completely.

[from the journal of Early Goddard]

08 March, 1858

    The day grew long while I slept and evefall will soon be upon us. I will not move Mam and Ada back into the dugout. I know what must be done with them, and to spare Enis the sight of their disposal, perhaps it shall be up to me to see that it is done, such that we shall be ready to escape for Lawrence at the first instant it is safe to do so. I know that I may not survive this last duty, but I have faith that we Goddards shall one day be reunited, be it in this world or in the next.

08 March, 1858
Physician's Journal

William is gone without a trace.

In the middle of the night I found and fell upon some Savages in their camp, and there I killed seven. An eighth fled and I tracked him and brought him down with my Bowie as he tried to dig with his hands into a bluff. This unfortunate Creature I hobbled by slashing the ropes of his heels, then employed the butt of my musket to break the both of his arms. In this pitiful condition I thereby questioned him at length and leisure on the whereabouts of William. He spoke not a few words of the Queen's English, and I had no understanding of his tongue, so this useless organ I removed from his mouth and devoured in front of him; a sight I ensured should be his last by carving out the both of his heathen eyes.

At dawn's break, I returned then to find the Goddards asleep in their bunker at Shiloh Swales, and there I promptly fired one ball into the chest of that fool, Marshall Goddard. The boy Enis awoke and dealt me my first wound in battle when he fired his musket at my throat. Most of the pellets I swallowed [illegible due to stains] did not much harm me. But he then fled me across the open fields and did escape, as my own musket was already discharged. I finished Marshall with my Bowie in such a manner as I would hope the Savages deem a fitting penance for his act of war against those peaceful Indians afield. Damn the Goddards, and damn the Daemon in their company.

I dressed the ragged hole in my throat with strips of Marshall's clothing, rested there in the bunker for a while, then charged my weapons and walked into Shiloh Swales with a mind to deprive the rest of the Goddard clan of their lives. But I found them all to be gone. There were signs in the snow where two bodies had been dragged and laid onto the ground. It appears to be Luretia who finally joined her daughter in death, and 'twas the elder son, Early, who must have loaded them into a cart and hauled their corpses westward, out onto the open plains. Had I not fought the Indians last night, they would surely have spotted the boy and his wagon and butchered him for his trouble. I reckon he is headed for a secret burial ground, a location I have yet to record.

08 March, 1858
Physician's Journal

Four hours I have trailed him, keeping low in the grass several leagues behind him. Never have I traversed or hunted in land so flat as this. I am a woodland beast, accustomed to the cover of forests, hills and hollers. Here there is no cover but yellow grass barely taller than a dog's shoulder. So much exposure must be unwholesome to the human mind, for so many who have settled here have gone mad and deprived their Selves and Others of their lives.

Here a pack of coyotes flanks me, so I give pause to let them pass. These beasts have no interest in me, their hunter brethren. I shall drift behind these prairie wolves and use their forms to cover my own. Should they reach the boy before me, I shall not begrudge them their prize. I shall sit at a distance and watch them enjoy it.

Here stopped again to record an extraordinary sight. In precisely the direction in which the Goddard boy is traveling, a great flock of living creatures did erupt from the ground to spill across the twilit sky. Bats or birds, I presume them to be, in an aggregation so numerous as to defy any estimate of their numbers. I say, the Airth disgorged this columnar swarm for nigh twelve minutes until the last of the winged creatures trailed up into the stars.

Perhaps the cavern from which these creatures emerged is in fact the burial site to which the Goddard boy is headed. Though there is no mountain in sight, our Agent once told us of a small vent in the Airth that is home to many bats; 'twas a shaft to the seas of the underworld, he said, used since time's beginning as a convenient grave to dispose of the dead.

Here I stop again at Evefall to strike up my little lantern, and by its dim light, record the fantastic commotion I now behold. The pack of coyotes engages the Goddard boy, such that he is forced to abandon his cart and flee out into the plains. But the dogs do not chase him; they drive him off and converge upon those corpses strapped to the wagon. Look at them growling and rending while the Goddard boy shouts and hurls his balls of snow. I must admit that I am much amused by this chaos, and by what seems a fitting end to those cherished corpses.

[illegible due to stain] rising up from the meat wagon with a terrific shriek, standing straight as twin planks, and the prairie wolves are all a scattering! Good God, and from the sight of his sister, Early flees, but the plains offer no escape for this one. He is doomed. She seems to glide after him through the long grass, claws outstretched and shroud a flowing--a perfect huntress! And it is over. I heard only the Goddard boy's single cry as she fastened herself upon him, and the two of them fell together into the grass. She has him, at last.

There now, poor Lurie lacks the vigour for the chase. She appears drunk, stupefied by the encroaching prairie wolves that seem to sense the weakness within her. One has the sleeve of her shroud! And another at the hem! They take her down, the monster, into their heaving huddle of bloody fur, all wrenching and pulling. They scatter now and then as she shrieks and lashes out at them, but promptly reconvene. There is no hope for this Revenant, this foul Consumptive, whose brief life shall be commemorated by naught but a paragraph in this journal.

Ada has risen again from her feast, her shroud smeared with the prints of her brother's hands. She is not finshed. Are you, Ada? I see you looking this way. You sense that I am here, and I sense your hunger through the coldness of your stare. But I have something that affrights you, do I not? You disappear into the grass, but I see you there, Ada, much closer now. I see the glow of your eyes. Circle my ring of light, you and the coyotes both, evil Ada, perfect huntress, queen of the bloodthirsty beasts, until my oil runs dry and the wick begins to flicker--and what then? What ever shall we do until dawn? I see you've sloughed your burial shroud. Feel the prairie wind blowing through your hair? I do. You are so beautiful in moonlight, but I know what you are. I could shoot you where you stand, and you know that. You see my pistol, and some part of you remembers what pistols can do, but you fear not my weapon because you know that I shall not draw it *against you. We understand each other in that small way, as beasts common to the same lonely charter understand the private language of their kind. Keep circling me. Keep circling me, considering my eyes with every pass, until the oil in our shared lantern burns low. When it dies, you shall come to know this old hunter completely.*

[journal end]

PART FIVE OF SIX:

THE LAST MAN'S CLUB

The boy could hear Pap's snores groaning through the darkness all the way to the foot of the drive, just as soon as he'd stepped out of the Model T. The boy sighed, and shook his head. All the care he'd taken to be so stealthy now seemed like it might've been a big waste of energy. Anything less than a gunshot four inches from his ear wasn't apt to wake that old fool from his cadaverous slumber, and drunk as Pap had been the night before, it would probably take him another day or two to fully recover. Drinking was one vice that no longer appealed to the boy, not in the smallest way. After his little ride with Enis Goddard, he'd come to regard corn whiskey as something of a devilish nostrum. The small amount he'd consumed on that strange afternoon had imparted a lingering bitterness, if only by its association to worse things.

The boy wrapped the stack of old journals in a burlap sack. Slinging the load over his shoulder, he quietly closed the door of the Model T. Pap balked his clandestine activity with a tremendous snort that should've choked an ordinary man. The boy wasn't sure where exactly he was going to hide the journals from his Pap until he'd found an opportunity to speak privately with J.P. With any luck, he'd be able to use those books as bargaining chips in order to win some adult confidence to his side of the line that separated men from boys. The boy reckoned J.P. would be pleased to reclaim his property. Those journals weren't "donated" to the Historical Guild by the Cobb family, as those raiders had suggested on their label that they'd slapped atop J.P.'s cedar trunk. That property had been stolen, and the boy had overheard enough rumors about the night it was taken from them to intuit that the trunk was filled not with history, but with evidence of the evil simmering just beneath the surface of their community.

Dawn's silver edge teased the eastern sky. This was the coldest hour of the day. The boy shivered, as the lonely keening of a meadowlark pierced the gloom far and wide across the flatlands. As the boy made his way up the drive, burlap sack swinging from the end of his arm, he observed scads of bats flitting through that hem between worlds divided by the light of the sun. Probably an hour before sunup. If it weren't for Pap's terrible snores, the distant rumble of the Rainmaker's howitzers, already shelling Rolla's skies with payloads of false promise, it might've been the start to a peaceful day. But by the active feel of things, like spinning gears in a grand machine driven by the flow of collective energy, this was a day harried from lazy beginnings into something of greater significance.

"Working some awful late hours around here, ain't ye?"

The boy dropped his sack of books at the sound of J.P.'s gravelly voice. His eyes searched the shadows. The pounding of his heart snatched the coattails of every breath in his throat, jerking each one short. There was some sizable trouble barreling his way before the goddamned day had even begun. His first order of business had been to seek out J.P., but his neighbor had managed to beat him to it, catching him totally off-guard, making him look like nothing more than a common thief of his neighbor's private property. The boy felt like a mangy coyote with a chicken dangling from its jaws, caught cowering in a rifle's crosshairs.

"Where you been all night?"

The boy could discern him now, sitting cross-legged on the east side of the homestead, facing that distant promise of a rising sun. This was a strange hour for paying a visit, to say the least. J.P. and Martha Cobb were rarely ever seen apart. They travelled everywhere together. They were regarded as a well-mannered couple who were never made anyone uncomfortable, or dropped by on folks uninvited. His presence at this hour made the boy have to wonder if the man had been up all night drinking.

Loathe to say a word that might be twisted back against him, the boy didn't reply. He snatched up his burlap sack, and resumed slogging up the drive with a glum resignation that seemed to add weight his extremities, causing his feet to drag through the dust, his body to sway from side to side. However, as he drew nearer the dark sentinel outside his home, a spark of resent kindled his guilt into a hotter sort of emotion. Here was nothing more than a nosy neighbor squatting on his property at a preposterous hour, questioning him, bullying him, just like his Pap.

The boy swaggered up to the seated man. He dropped his sack of books at J.P.'s feet, and then folded his thin arms across his chest. Overhead, bats wheeled through the starlight.

"Didn't hear me? I asked where ye been."

"Out," the boy replied, flatly.

"Nothing good ever happened to anybody after midnight. You shouldn't be worrying your Pap like this, running around all hours of the night like a damned cat in heat."

"Does he sound worried to you?" the boy replied, sharpening his tone, as Pap's awful snores threatened to collapse the earthen walls of their home. He'd never sassed J.P. before, but then, he'd never had a reason to give him any lip. It suddenly felt like that line that separated menfolk and boys had just been crossed, but he wasn't sure which of them had done the crossing. On one hand, it felt exhilarating to stand on equal ground against another grown fellow, but on the other, it was pretty darned scary, like he was still just a child acting tough, who was maybe on the verge of getting a whipping.

"What ye got in that bag?"

"How 'bout you open it, and see for yourself."

The boy shifted his feet, suddenly uncomfortable by the tension he'd created. He couldn't see the whites of J.P.'s eyes, but he could feel the dark energy of his glare. After a few awkward moments, the old cowboy lurched upright. The boy unfolded his skinny arms. When J.P. stepped close enough that the boy could smell his musk, feel a wave of heat rolling off of his broad chest, he felt compelled to fold his arms back up again.

"I asked, what ye got in that bag."

"Books," the boy blurted.

"What kinder books?"

The boy retrieved the bag. Extending his arm, he held it up to J.P. "Yours. All the ones got stolen from your folks by the Guild. I brought them back for you."

"My Great-Grandpappy's journal?"

"Yes, sir, and a few more beyond that."

J.P. dropped his gaze to the dirt for a moment, and then lifted his head slowly back up again. "Thought your Pap made it clear you wasn't allowed to set foot in that old school house ever again."

There was no equal ground at all. The boy was still regarded as a child. J.P. let the sack of books dangle in the air until the boy's arm started to quiver. At the instant his arm began to fall, J.P.'s thick hand shot, and seized the burlap bag by the flaccid folds of its throat.

"Hard of hearing, are ye? Or hard of learning, one? I thought your Pap taught you a hard lesson the last time ye—"

"I read all them journals. I read every damned one of them, cover to cover. I know everything that's went on between the Goddard clan and your'n."

"Do ye now?"

"Yes, sir," the boy said, clearing his throat, "all of it, and beyond that, I'm the only one in this whole danged

world who knows what really happened to Enis Goddard."
He unfolded his arms, planted his hands on his hips, and
stared up into J.P.'s eyes. "Bet you'd like to hear that story,
wouldn't ye? I might even decide to tell it. But first, you got
to tell me who won that last fight between your Great-
Grandpappy and Ada Goddard? You tell me whichever
one of them two came out of that scrape alive, and then
maybe I'll tell you what happened to Enis Goddard. Deal?"

Inside, Pap snorted like a great, chuckling hog. He
then wheezed a lungful of dusty air through his pursed lips.
The dull thunder of artillery rumbled over the wastelands.
Stirring thistles began to whisper in the breeze.

"Ye done murdered him yourself, I'd reckon," J.P.
said, his voice dropping to a basal timbre.

Stunned by the old cowboy's impossible intuition, the
boy took an involuntary step backwards. He suddenly felt
a little faint. His heart resumed its wild hammering as the
swarms of bats circled closer, wheeling over the tops of their
heads with every swoop. Seemed as though the creatures
were drawn to the dark subject of their conversation,
almost as though they were eavesdropping.

"I've been watching you, ye know." J.P. strode forward one step, to reclaim the distance the boy created in his
retreat. "Been watching over your homestead nightly, every
night since Black Sunday."

"You?" the boy stammered. "You're the one I'd been
hearing, prowling around out here every night?"

"Darned right."

"But I figured it was—"

"I seen what Enis Goddard was up to. He had you and
your Pap both lined up in his sights. Your Pap already lost

enough to that son-of-a-bitch when he took your Mam from ye. I wasn't about to let my buddy lose anything more."

"The heck do you mean?" The boy could feel all the blood draining from his face until his ears started to buzz. His lips went numb. For a moment, he thought he might get sick. "You mean ... you're saying that God killed my—"

"Ah-ah." J.P. raised a finger. He shushed him, glancing upward as a passing bat swooped by his ear. "Too dangerous to talk here. Need to go elsewhere. Got something we need to do anyhow, before sunup. Best go wake up your Pap, tell him to pull his boots on."

"Hang on a minute," the boy said, shaking his head from side to side. "We ain't going to drag my Pap into this." His eyes then widened when he noticed what was propped against the side of their house, right beside the spot where J.P. had been sitting. It was a crossbow. A crossbow and quiver of cedar bolts. The boy frowned at this added peculiarity to an already strange scene.

"Time you start trusting your ol' Pap. Quit fearing him. Get to know more about him, as a man," J.P. said, his voice lowered nearly to a whisper. "After all, your Pap is the best vampire killer in the Club."

———

The Model T peeled off the road, fishtailing through drifts of moon dust. Thistles slapped and clawed at the undercarriage. Pap wore a solemn expression as he veered along the dusky draw that trailed into the ghost town of Vorhees. Still mostly dark, the sun hadn't yet pierced the eastern horizon, but a distant Osage hedgerow had just begun to glitter before the hint of a new dawn that was now just minutes away. The Model T rolled to a stop alongside the old windmill pad that the boy had discovered the night before.

Pap and J.P. popped their door handles simultaneously. The two men stepped out of the vehicle and into the ashen wasteland, squinting in the dust that was already beginning to blow. The boy slid across the seat after his Pap. He dropped out the driver's side door, and slipped past the older men. Wandering Wesley's ratty sack was still slumped behind the weeds. The dead lantern protruded from a pedestal of dust with a sort of quiet solidarity. But the main article of interest, being a pair of snapped-off legs once worn by a missing hermit, were nowhere to be seen. After circling the area a time or two, the boy stopped pacing, placed both his hands atop his head, and scowled at the featureless ruins. Somewhere in the distance, a cow lowed.

"I don't get it," he said, as his Pap and J.P. sidled up to the pad, "they were right there. I swear it."

"Sometimes things can l-look different at night, than during the day."

"No. They were sticking up right over there. Right there!"

"Coyotes," J.P. said, spitting into the dirt. "Hell, they might've even killed him. They'll sure gang up on a bogged bull if they get hungry enough. Wouldn't put it past a bunch of them to do the same to a crippled old man."

"You don't get it." The boy strode to the spot where he remembered the pair of blunt shins poking straight up from the dust, and he turned to face the two men. "Them legs were standing perfectly upright. Not scattered all around. There wasn't a big ol' bloody mess like the kind a pack of coyotes always make. Nah, these were sliced clean off, neat as can be, like he was snapped right off them so darned fast that his old feet didn't even tip over." The boy squinted up at the steely sky. "It was like, something come swooping right down onto him — something *big* — and chomped him clean off above the ankles."

J.P. grunted, one eye flicking skyward, then back down to earth again.

Pap glanced at J.P., then swiveled his head toward the boy. He placed a hand on the boy's shoulder. "Don't know if it's worth worrying too much over this one."

"But it had to be something that done it."

"Or maybe s-someone, playing some devilish tricks."

J.P. shook his head. "I got to side with your Pap on this one. Had to be a bad man, or a group of them, come up on him in the night. Planted them feet when they were done, and the coyotes surely ran off with them. Whatever it was, wind and dust has covered their trail." J.P. sighed, and stared at the dust for a few moments. "Day's about to break. We'd better get after it, if we're going to do this today."

"I'd r-reckon so."

The boy just watched as J.P. loped over to the edge of the windmill pad, where he began kicking away drifted dust. Once he'd located the pad's edge, he followed it with the pointed toe of his boot until his foot clunked against something that looked like an old U-bolt hitch. Upon unearthing this, he dropped to his knees, swept around with his hands, until he fished up a rusty tow chain that was attached to it. "Here," J.P. said, offering the end of the chain to the boy, "go wind this around the frame."

The boy obeyed, dragging a much longer chain than he'd expected from beneath eight inches of powdery dust to the back end of the Model T. There, he crouched, reeving the chain tightly around the anchor point. Once finished, he gave the chain a couple of good tugs to be sure that it wasn't going to slip off. He looked to J.P., who replied with a nod of approval.

"Hop on into driver's seat, but don't do anything else until I tell ye."

"Yes, sir."

The boy hustled around to the driver's side, popped the door, and clambered into the seat. He glanced over his shoulder when he felt the vehicle sag beneath the added weight of the two men, who'd both clambered up onto the Model T's rear fenders. He guessed they'd done this to give the automobile some better traction in the loose dust.

"Ye ready?"

"Yes, sir!"

"Nice and easy, then. Go ahead and ease her forward."

The boy reached for the throttle on the steering column. He edged it forward. The automobile crept ahead until the length of tow chain rose from the dust, tightening between the frame and the windmill pad. The eastern sky had just begun to blush. Wouldn't be long before the sun crested with its blinding effervescence.

"Go on and give her a little gas now, nice and easy."

The boy pushed the throttle lever steadily forward until he could feel the Model T straining against the tow chain. The engine ramped up into a moan. There came a great spray of dust from beneath the rear tires. The two men covered their eyes and turned their heads. The boy grinned, goosing the throttle a little harder. A fountain of filth showered down over the tops of the old cowboys. The Model T heaved, fishtailed, and finally found purchase on something beneath the dust. They began to roll forward, with a terrible scrape of a concrete slab sliding over limestone footings. The pad was moving. Dust was pulled from the air, funneling into a widening mouth in the earth by some force of subterranean suction.

"Alright, whoa!" J.P. was waving his hand back and forth. "That's good. Let her off, if you would."

The three stood shoulder to shoulder, gawping down a limestone staircase that seemed to drop straight down into Hell. The boy shivered in a waft of cold air that was infused with the reek of decomposition. His hand rose to cup the lower half of his face as he took a step back from the fetid mouth of the cavern.

"Nothing keeps a good secret quite like an ol' desert," J.P. said, narrowing his eyes at the yawning shaft. "Dig down thirty feet just about anywhere around here, and you'll tap right into a whole labyrinth that's never once been touched by the light of the sun. Some believe if ye dig far enough there's a whole ocean down there, and I can't say I doubt it."

The boy nodded, still covering his face.

"Used to be an old church house sitting here, years ago, and down there was the old storm shelter. But this old hole in the ground had plenty of stories to tell before them stairs was ever carved, before that church was built atop it. It'd been here for ages, before any white man ever thought to repurpose it." J.P. frowned, stroking the whiskers of his chin. "Old folks used to tell that this hole was once a geyser, an open shaft running straight down to the aquifer that dried up thousands of years ago. The Indians found it before the whites ever came along. We know that much. Ancient Indians. Mound builders. Ones who settled here long before the Kiowa or the Comanche. We don't know much about them folks, but we know this here was a sacred place. Place of dark ritual and sacrifice. All them bones was still down there when my granddad, William Cobb, had the steps carved, and the church built atop it. Served a whole lot of purposes for humankind, this old cavern, but after the Goddard gang rode through here, slaughtered everyone, burned the church and all of Vorhees to the ground— well, my own daddy found a new purpose for this hole, altogether."

"That's what happened to Vorhees?" the boy asked, squinting up at J.P. "God burned it down?"

J.P. did not reply. He just stared down into the depths of the hollow with the hardest sort of resolve that a man can gather into his brow. The boy was beginning to understand that a blood feud was to blame for everything. A feud, festering with enough hatred to fuel a secret war between three generations of Cobbs and Goddards that had managed to catch his own family in the crossfire. The old journals accounted well enough for those first seeds sown to be propagated into a dark harvest of lives. It was J.P.'s Great-Grandpappy who fired the first shot. Justified or not, it was Dr. Beauregard "Buckshot" Cobb who'd drawn first blood when he made his fateful journey to Shiloh Swales, and there, discovered the Goddard family's secret.

Based on all he'd written down in his journal, he'd seemed to truly believe that for all his personal sacrifice, for all the lives of the loved ones he'd lost along the trail, it was the Goddard family who had deceived him. For that sin, he'd turned on the Goddards with a vengeance. In a show of vigilante justice not much seen beyond the close of the nineteenth century, the old hunter had singlehandedly lynched an entire family.

On the drive out to Vorhees, J.P.'s jaw had finally loosened, and he confirmed the boy's suspicions that in the end, only little Enis Goddard had managed to escape the slaughter at Shiloh Swales. It was believed that he'd fled to Utah, where he likely attended Mormon schooling, and grew up to become a successful man. Once the High Plains had been cleared of Indians, squatting slavers, border ruffians, and the anti-Mormon sentiment was quelled, Enis slipped quietly back down into Kansas with an aim to purchase Shiloh Swales, to take ownership of those ruins where his brief childhood had come to a bloody end. The horrors he'd experienced amidst those domed hills had undoubtedly haunted him his whole darned life, and you couldn't hardly blame the man for wanting to control the chaos of his past by civilizing the blighted spot of land that had consumed his whole family. However, God couldn't possibly have expected that after all of those years, his past wasn't finished with him. Not just yet. It was waiting for him, in fact, in the form of the very man who'd butchered his whole family—at least, was left of him.

"Like I said, my Great-Grandpappy won that final showdown, but not before she delivered him a single bite, right there on the side of his neck," J.P. said, tapping the side of his throat. "In a lifetime of warring, that one bite from Ada Goddard was the worst blow my Great-Grandpappy could have ever been dealt, because it clipped his wings, ye see. It robbed him of his freedom. That venom was a liquid curse injected into his veins. He was a man who loved nothing better than traveling the world's wildest places, but the curse bound him for all eternity to a barren patch of country that he hated more than any other place. Blamed that on the Goddards, of course, just as he'd rightfully blamed them for the life of his best buddy, his daughter-in-law, and his two little granddaughters, Emily and Ester. My Great-Grandpappy lost everything he ever had to the Goddard clan, along with everything he might've had, all for trying to help them. When Enis grew up and came back from Utah, Great-Grandpappy hunted his ass down. Thought it only fair he return that Goddard family curse right back to its rightful heir, and that's when the monster you murdered was born."

The boy stared down into the shaft of fetid blackness. He didn't much care for the word "murder" used in regard to what had happened to God, but he didn't much feel like arguing semantics. The flow of cold air past his face gave the distinct impression that he was looking right down into something's throat, and the drafts that he felt on his skin were the thing's soured breaths. He realized that he was the only one covering his nose. With some reluctance, he lowered his hand. "What's down there," he whispered, "at the bottom of them stairs?"

"Family secrets," J.P. said, "of the darkest kind."

Pap placed a gentle hand on the boy's shoulder.

"My Granddad, William Cobb, was mayor of Vorhees when God came riding into town with a gang of blood-suckers," J.P. said, solemnly. "Whereas most folks would hate the idea of being turned into a damned vampire, God actually seemed to enjoy it. It wasn't never a curse to him. It was a gift. God learned to ride the storms, moving whenever them dusters rolled through, and blocked out the sun." J.P. nodded. "God was coming for my Granddad, that much was sure, but one life wasn't going to be enough to satisfy a bloodthirsty gang. My Granddad and most everyone else in the town of Vorhees all met with the same terrible end. Every building that stood here went up in an inferno that folks could see as far away as Liberal. That old hermit, Wandering Wesley, was just a boy about your age the night it happened. He survived because the Goddard gang never found this old staircase, and to this day, no bloodsucker has ever found it—except for the ones we put down there."

"Welcome to the Vorhees Z-Zoo."

"What?" The boy shot a horrified look at his Pap.

J.P. lowered himself to one knee at the top of the staircase, and he hollered straight down into the blackness. "Hello, down there! It's me, J.P. I've brought a young friend to meet you, but you ain't going to do him no harm. Ye hear me?"

The boy's heart drummed inside his hollow. He could hear the chug and rush of cold blood in his ears. "We ain't really going down there," he said, looking pleadingly up to his Pap, "not you and me."

"No," Pap replied, averting his eyes, "j-just you."

"I say, are ye fit for company?" J.P. snatched hold of the boy's upper arm, and he held him fast. "I think you'd be awful pleased to meet this young fellow. He's the newest member of the Last Man's Club. He's a damned vampire killer! Done killed ol' Enis Goddard with his bare hands!"

Pop-eyed and palpitating, the boy dug in his heels. Although the grip around his arm was not painfully tight, it was evident by the steely sinews of a fist forged by a lifetime of field labor that there was no chance of pulling loose until J.P. was good and ready to release him. If he'd a mind to do it, J.P. could've probably yanked his arm clean out of its socket, and whopped him right over the head with it. The boy stopped tugging. His knees went limp when down below, a gaseous hiss of expelled breath set some cobwebs to swaying. It was not the hole itself that was doing the breathing. It was something else. Something down there in it.

J.P. looked down at the boy, nodding, as if to signal that it was time to move, but the usual twinkle in his eye was missing. His glare was a hard one, dried of any splash of emotion. "I believe someone's ready to meet you." Pinching at his nose, he rose, still clenching the boy's arm, and he took one shaky step down into the hole. Below, something shuffled toward the base of the staircase with evident anticipation. Loose pebbles clattered through the gloom. J.P hesitated on the first tread of the staircase, gaping down into the void. He licked his lips. "Now, you're going to behave yourself, aren't you?"

Only silence from down in the underworld.

J.P. looked back at the boy. He allowed a hesitant nod, as he took another step downward. When the boy faltered, he gave a brusque tug to his skinny arm. "Straighten up, now. We only got but a minute, here. Once that morning sun rises, we've done missed our chance."

"Our chance for what?" The pitch of the boy's voice seemed to have risen two octaves.

"To speak with the dead."

The Last Man's Club was something more than just a labor union. The boy was beginning to understand that, now. It was a clandestine force of farmers and ranchers who assembled for the general purpose of protecting their land, their livelihood, their communities—and it was becoming evident that their common enemies were not exclusively crooked bankers.

"The Last Man's Club was formed after the Goddard gang's attack on Vorhees," J.P. explained, as they descended the crumbling staircase. "The menfolk of neighboring communities saddled up their horses, and they chased that band of bloodsuckers way out into the heart of no-man's land. They lost track of them in the wasteland, but they didn't figure those rogues had a snowball's chance in Hell of making it to any sort of cover before sunrise. Turned out, they figured wrong. Years passed without a sign of Enis Goddard," J.P. whispered, ushering the boy down the lime-stone staircase, one weathered tread at a time, "but those weren't years to celebrate. The land itself seemed to suffer and die. Drought set in. Black dusters became the regular weather, until all the filth in the air forever covered the sun. Crops withered. Cattle died. Nothing grew. That's the world you were born into. That's when Enis Goddard returned, from wherever he'd been hiding."

J.P. brushed aside a curtain of cobwebs that clung to his hand like a tattered, white glove. He smeared the silk on the hip of his trousers. "Seemed he'd become a wiser sort of bloodsucker than the ol' gangster he used to be. Had a plan. Seized control of the local government, brought telephone line technology into no-man's land, and one can only begin to imagine why. Since you murdered him, the Club's begun to see signs. Something's festering. Something way down below is wanting badly to come up, lurking down there under no-man's land for a thousand years, or better. The ancient Indians knew about it. Yes, sir. It's something worse than a vampire—something big."

"J.P.," the boy pleaded, pulling back against the flesh manacle that dragged him deeper into the craw of Hell's throat, "the sun's coming up!"

"That's alright. We'll still have a minute or two."

"Ain't it going to kill them, though?"

A chuff of air escaped the blackness with a maleficent hiss. The boy heard the scrape of claws against limestone. Never in his life had he felt such a powerful aversion to any situation. Whatever was scuttling around down there seemed far too anxious to receive him to be harboring any kind intentions. J.P. yanked at his upper arm, and a terrible thought crossed the boy's mind. What if he'd crossed some sort of a line? What if he'd learned too much, become labeled as a potential threat to the Club in his tireless pursuit of knowledge?

"Darned right sunlight will kill them. No matter, though. Once the sun sets, they rise back up again."

"J.P., you don't mean to leave me down—"

"Beheading!" J.P. wrenched the boy around in front of him as they reached the bottom of the staircase. "A stake rammed right their black heart! That's how to kill a vampire completely."

"Wait!" the boy exclaimed. "There's another way. I know of a better way!"

Gripping the boy by both of his arms, J.P. pulled him close, and squinted at him through one mean eye. "How'd you do it? Tell me, damn it! How the hell did you manage to kill that bloodsucker?"

The boy struggled to recall that chaotic scene of fire, a Comanche arrow, a mauling dog, and a bolt of lightning. He'd never been positive about which of those factors had actually been lethal, robbing God of his second life. But whichever had done him in, it was the only bit of information about Draculas that he, and he alone, still possessed. Eyes bulging, gritting his teeth, he ducked away from J.P.'s ravenous glare, hoping that whatever knowledge he withheld might be worth consideration for sparing his life.

"Fair enough. Have it your way." J.P. turned to the cavern, and bellowed into the icy blackness. "Ye down here?" Great plumes of steam billowed from his mouth. "Come on out!"

"Fire!" the boy shrieked.

"What's that?"

"Fire. It was fire that killed God."

J.P. nodded, sticking out his lower lip. "Yeah, I'd forgotten that one. They go up like a damned tinderbox when you light 'em, don't they?" A broad grin spread across his weathered face. "Your Pap used to dip his arrows into a jar of moonshine, light them up right before letting one fly. Them bloodsuckers would darned near explode when he'd hit them just right with one of those things." J.P. chuckled softly. "Truth is, I think your Pap just liked a reason to carry around a jar of moonshine."

The boy's gaze fell to the cave floor. The only card he'd been holding had just turned out to be trash. Seemed like there was nothing he'd ever learned on his own that J.P and his Pap didn't already know. Now, he almost felt a little sheepish for mistaking his Pap for an old fool. Never once had he doubted the man's durability. Pap was as hard as cast iron. Not even Enis Goddard had been able to break or bend him.

One after another, God had bullied his way over the sections, intimidating farmers, snatching up easements for pennies on the dollar until at last his progress came to a dead halt when that unstoppable force found itself pitted against an immovable object. That object was Lionel Crow, otherwise known as Pap, who came to be celebrated as a working man's hero when the months rolled by without a settlement to their standoff. Despite God's mounting threats, despite his so-called legal backing by his blood-sucker's branch of the local government, Pap refused to budge. Something was going to have to give, and everyone knew it. That something finally gave under the light of a harvest moon, while the boy and Pap were out shocking rows of the thinnest wheat they'd ever raised. The Goddard Gang paid a little visit to their homestead, where his poor Mam was home all alone.

"You remember Darla? Darla Crow?" J.P. hollered into the blackness. "You were awfully fond of that woman while she was alive. Do ye remember her?"

The boy could hardly believe what he was hearing. His Mam, his own Mam, had been friends with—whatever was down here. Had anything in his life ever been what it had seemed?

"Well, this young man is Darla's only son. I thought you'd maybe like to meet him. Enis Goddard took Darla's life, and this boy went and killed that son-of-a-bitch in return."

The shadows seemed to gather, smoldering in the cavern's darkest recess like a sentient wad of dark energy, but whatever it was had substantial mass. Grit shifted beneath its feet. As the boy's eyes adjusted to the lightless environment, he discerned things stiff and articulated scattered about the cave floor. White knobs protruded from flags of desiccated flesh. Clawing hands, frozen in desperate, supplicating gestures, forever pleading to the aversive gods who'd forsaken them. Beyond a tumulus of skulls, the boy could just catch the glimmer of a pair of amber eyes. He knew the fire that burned within them, and those flames seemed to remember him.

"I see you hiding back there," J.P. said. "We only got but a minute to speak before that morning sun turns ye back to a heap of bones, and I'm afraid we'd best talk now, as there might not come another tomorrow. The bats are in flight. I can feel it stirring, and I know you can feel it too. Something old has done awakened. We aim to take the fight to it, but we'll need your help. It's safe to come up topside again, now that God's dead. Would you like that?" J.P. smiled, and licked his lips. "Wouldn't you like to come upstairs tonight, and see the moon and the stars? We need you to come on up, show us the way out to the Comanche Vent."

Dark lids narrowed the coyote eyes to burning slits. With spiderlike fluidity, the dark form clambered horizontally over bones, inverted, gliding on its back on all fours. The boy stood hypnotized by the unnatural movement of a thing human only in shape, a thing possessed by a presence that utilized its cadaverous vehicle in ways for which a human body was never designed. Dead flesh obeyed, rafting the alien entity soundlessly over reefs of skulls, thickets of femurs, outcrops of jagged ribs. It wasn't until a skull took a tumble to clatter woodenly across the limestone that the boy reeled in a spasm of electric terror. J.P.'s grip on his arms tightened, holding him fast, until his boots were kicking in the air.

"Damn it, settle down! Ain't going to hurt ye long as you're here with me."

With the scratch of outgrown nails, the shuffle of ragged clothing, it came dragging ropes of dead hair through the dust. But it was that stench, that sulfurous brimstone stink, burning his nostrils like the memory of corn whiskey upon his tongue. The thing rotated its ruined head, lolling its tongue through rattlesnake fangs. The boy swung his legs up around J.P.'s midsection, and wrapped his arms around the man's leathery neck. Had he been a tree, he'd have climbed him all the way to the top.

"Whenever you're ready to get off me," J.P. said, with an aggravated grunt, prying the boy's fingers loose, "I'd like to introduce you to somebody. This here is my Great-Grandpappy, Dr. Beauregard 'Buckshot' Cobb."

The boy swiveled his head, stole a quick peek at the abomination behind him. The thing was rising to its feet. J.P. cleared his throat with a growl of insistence. The boy loosened his knotted legs, unlatched his arms, and regretfully slid back down onto his feet. Still pressed against J.P., he found the courage to turn, and face it.

The creature was shorter than he might've expected, but his diminutive stature didn't seem disproportionate, or in any way unnatural. By the low clearance of framed doorways in Eden's oldest homes, it had always seemed evident to the boy that folks just didn't grow quite as tall back then as they did now. That's when the gravity of the moment seized firm hold of the boy's mind. A whole century was clipped right out of history's great reel, and Dr. Cobb stood there like a splice in time's severed ends. Here was a living relic, an author of dusty journals penned in a bygone window of time.

The vampire smeared his palm against his shabby overcoat, and extended the boy his clawed hand. Eyes aglow from within the wild tussock of hair that framed a filthy face, the creature's lips began to quiver, as if struggling to remember the old contortions that had once produced speech. Beneath a slathering of black cave dirt, its throat rose and fell, drawing the boy's attention to a great mess of scar tissue that he recognized as the result of a musket blast dealt him by none other than little Enis Goddard. Next to these remnants was a set of puncture wounds, two-inches apart, not unlike the bite of a large rattlesnake.

"I extend my condolences," the monster whispered, venom dribbling down through the fibers of his beard, "to ye family."

The boy replied with a single nod. What could he say? How could he thank this creature for its sentiments when he'd only just learned that the century of bloodshed that had consumed his own Mam was this monster's fault? Cain leered before him, forever marked with twin holes as the fountainhead of a dark legacy. J.P. nudged him from behind, and the boy realized that the monster's extended hand was still hanging emptily in the air.

"I thank ye kindly," the monster hissed, as a shaft of dawn's first rays lit upon its sallow face, "for putting the last Goddard to rest."

The fiery glow of its coyote eyes began to flicker and wane, as sunshine's touch snuffed whatever kindled the animating presence of a long-dead husk. The boy finally reached out to grip the clawed hand of the vampire. As the creature gave him a frigid shake, he could feel the flesh withering beneath its skin.

"What's ye name, boy?" the vampire asked, as desiccating layers sloughed the underlying carriage of bones in gray veils of falling dust. Those dying embers blackened in their hollows. The skeletal hand relaxed its grip, curling inward toward the wrist. The bushy head lolled back on its rotten stump, gawping skyward, as its jaw dropped open to emit that silent howl of the dead. "I say, what's ye na—"

The magical moment bridging time's shores suddenly collapsed, and a whole century flooded back into the gap. The boy released the shriveled hand, allowing the twisted form of a mummy to topple. A wake of dust unfurled, as the nearly weightless ruck of bones struck the limestone floor with a muffled clatter. Outside, a distant cow lowed.

PART SIX OF SIX:

BLOOD HARVEST

"How'd she die, Pap?" the boy asked, glancing across the seat of the Model T at the face of a father he hardly recognized anymore. It seemed that there were layers upon layers to this man, who wasn't half so simple as he might've seemed right up until the first rays of this morning's strange dawn. Pap looked harder, wiser than perhaps he'd ever looked before.

"I'd guess you remember that night well enough." Pap's gaze skewed sideways to the rolling dunes of moon dust that blanketed every acre of desert between Vorhees and Rolla. "You were a pretty young sprout, but you ain't liable to forget how we come home late from shocking wheat, and we found your Mam lying outside on the hill, right in the spot where we buried her, come morning."

"But she wasn't dead, Pap. She was still breathing when we found her. You told me she was sick, and I went off to bed thinking she'd get better."

"I maybe shouldn't have told you that." Pap's hand rose to wipe his nose, and then fell back into his lap with a lifeless smack. "I don't know. I wasn't thinking too clearly, at the time. But hell, it's hard to say what I ought to have told ye. This is a hard thing for me to have to remember. Hardest thing of all."

The boy glanced at his Pap, then back to the dusty road beyond the wheel. "I remember you carried her inside, laid her down on the bed. She was breathing awfully heavy, but she was alive. You told me she was sick, but when we woke up the next morning, she was gone. Just gone."

"I didn't lie to ye. She was sick. Deathly sick. She'd been bit, right here." Pap lifted his arm, and he tapped two hooked fingers against the inside of his wrist. "They could have k-killed her, but they didn't. Instead, they decided to be cruel." Pap turned to chill the boy with a hollowed glare that felt just as cold as any grave. "They left that part up to me."

"You?"

Pap nodded, and turned back to the window. He wiped the back of his hand beneath his eyes. "They always die by morning light. You remember how we found her the next day. Death had taken the color from her sweet face, robbed the shine from her loving eyes. She was g-gone. From the moment she got bit, your Mam was gone. I didn't exactly have to take her life. They'd already done took it. But, I did have to make sure she didn't come back."

The boy shook his head slowly from side to side. "We didn't have no funeral or nothing for her, Pap. Just buried her like a shot dog. Why didn't we give her a proper funeral?" The boy sniffed, blinking back the moisture that was beginning to cloud his eyes. "She deserved that, at least."

"There wasn't time for none of that, son. We couldn't invite a whole crowd of relatives and prying eyes into that situation. She'd been bit. Understand? She was going to turn. There ain't no cure for it, and the longer you put off the inevitable, the harder it gets. I've seen what can happen when folks hang on to a bit one, try to keep them around a while longer. It ain't no good. I wasn't about to let any of that happen under my roof. Wasn't going to put you at risk, or even let you suffer the sight of what was to come of her, at dusk. I'd be d-damned if you'd remember your Mam as being anything but the angel she was. But then, I guess I reckon I'll be damned anyhow, for doing what needed to be done."

The boy gritted his teeth. He clenched the wheel, twisting it between his fists. For years, he'd believed she'd just died peacefully in the night. To learn otherwise made him bite down on the insides of his cheeks until he tasted the salty copper of his own blood. It was bad enough to learn how she'd been attacked. He couldn't bear to imagine his Mam terrified, all alone, struggling against a gang of howling bloodsuckers in the light of a harvest moon. Wasn't fair. She'd done nothing to deserve that. But still, he didn't know how he was ever going to bring himself to look at his Pap the same way ever again, knowing that he was the one who'd put her down.

"How?" the boy choked.

"You really want to hear this?"

The boy nodded, grimacing, smearing away his tears.

"When we buried her, I was careful to set the point of that Osage cross right over her heart, just touching her chest, and we filled in all around it. You and I sat on that hilltop beside her grave when the work was finished. Sat there all day, you and I, and into the evening, when the three of us shared a sunset together, one last time. Remember that, do ye?"

The boy nodded, too choked up to be able to reply. That last sunset was burned as vividly into his memory as anything else he'd ever seen. Funny, he'd always liked to remember that evening as being one of the few moments in his life that he'd felt a strong bond with his Pap. But that moment had all been a lie. He wiped the streaming tears from the corners of his eyes.

"Come sundown, I sent you inside to get cleaned up for dinner. Once you'd gone into the house, I took up the sledge, said my last goodbye, and then I drove that Osage cross—" Pap nodded, smearing away tears of his own. "I done the right thing. She was stone dead when I done it. Didn't feel a thing. She died from a poisoned bite as Darla Crow, and she never became nothing else."

Twin oceans of rolling dust spumed in the wind, casting off grey forms the spirited over the road. The boy blinked, and cleared his throat. "But now that Enis is dead—being the feller who probably turned her into a vampire—haven't you ever start to wonder if maybe she ... you know?"

"Lord in Heaven, no!" Pap thumped the butt of his hand against the dashboard. "Don't even go thinking such kinder thoughts. For sure, don't go believing all the nonsense ye see in them moving picture shows, or reading in them d-damned monster books. That venom stops a beating heart forever, just as surely as any rattlesnake. If you get bit, you die. Only one way you're coming back, and it ain't the way ye used to be."

"I know you don't like my monster books, Pap, but if there's any truth to them stories, they all say that if ye kill the bloodsucker who bit ye, then it can cure you, turn you back."

"Back into what, son? Back into what? A heap of old bones with an Osage stake through the heart? What good can it do ye to think them kinder thoughts? Just accept it, son. She's gone."

"I do accept it! But maybe you ought to accept that ye didn't give me no kind of credit. Never have, either! Hell, I'd have wanted more'n anything to go out and help ye kill that sumbitch the same day if we thought there might've been a chance to save her!"

"I know ye would have, goddamn it, but I wasn't going to lose ye both in one day, and that's just exactly what would've come of it, had ye known."

"You can't know that."

"I can wager a best guess at it, anyhow. You were next on his list, son. I can promise you that. And you were all I had left in a world that seemed to have an awful thirst for our blood. What would you do, if it was just you and ye only boy against the whole damned world, and ye had but a few hours to decide?"

"I wouldn't need five minutes."

"Shit... wait 'til ye get a little older, and I'll ask ye the same question again."

Dust slithered across the road to Rolla in serpentine tendrils. Wind was picking up. A wall of darkness was shelving in the west, a playground for lightning that pulsed all through its black guts. Despite its bright beginnings, today was headed straight into the shitter. There was an argument flaring between the Rainmaker's howitzers, and what sounded like distant thunder. You could scarcely tell one from the other. If the skies actually decided to open right after three days of the Rainmaker's shelling, and some rain really fell... Lord have mercy, nobody would ever hear the end of it.

"What are we going to do?" the boy finally asked.

Pap just grunted.

It seemed that at last, after so many years of deception, he'd finally managed to wrangle the whole truth from two men who'd worked so tirelessly to keep it from him. It all seemed so ludicrous now, to think how much more his life had been endangered by being sheltered from the truth about a monster who'd have liked nothing more than a chance to carve out his liver. It angered him, in a way. He'd lived his whole life so naïve, so wrongfully imperiled. And what had changed? Despite all the new knowledge he'd managed to squeeze from those two, old stones, Pap was still set on keeping him in the dark, if there was even a plan at all.

"Can ye tell me where we're headed," the boy asked, "and why we left J.P. all alone back in Vorhees, sitting on his nuts beside his Great-Grandpappy's bones?"

"Headed to R-Rolla, like I told ye." Pap scowled, as if the answers to his questions were incredulously obvious. "J.P. will catch up with us later. This is all mostly his family business, anyhow. You and me, we're just kinder caught up in it."

"J.P. mentioned something else when he took me down them stairs."

"What's that?"

"Seemed pretty worried over something else. Something *worse* than any vampire—something *big*."

Pap shrugged, turning back to the passenger window.

"I read about that ol' Comanche Vent in them journals. Place where the old Injuns used to go and dump all the bodies of their dead."

"Mm-hm."

"Think that's where the *something bigger* is hiding?"

"Like I said, it's J.P.'s business. We're just lending him a hand, like a couple of good neighbors ought to."

"Ye think it might be the same thing that killed ol' Wandering Wesley?"

"Hell, I don't know n-nothing about any of that mess."

"Really? Nothing at all?" The boy gawped at his aversive Pap. "J.P. told me that you were the best vampire killer in the whole Club. Figured you'd be the one to know if there was something even worse out there than a damned vampire."

"You watch your cussing."

"J.P. said there might not even come another to-morrow. What the heck's he mean by that?"

Pap shrugged.

"You don't know, or you don't want to tell me?"

"See why we never tell you nothing?" Pap shot the boy a weird look, hoisting one eyebrow. "Ye ask too many damned questions."

———— ·•·◆·•· ————

The Rainmaker preached to his listless handful. By his third day of bombardment, they were all he had left. Mostly children, a few weary mothers, idled within earshot of his trailer. A game of marbles was underway down in a small clearing in the dust. The Rainmaker paced his flatbed, mouthing his bullhorn, clinging to his hat in the blustery wind. Near the army howitzers, hired hands loped about frowning over the crates of ammunition, clutching their reams of flapping orders that had evidently been devised by their wizardly employer to ensure that the precisely sequenced shells were delivered on schedule to their heavenly coordinates. By the confounded looks on all of their faces, it appeared as though the Rainmaker's science was made just difficult enough to comprehend that any failure to burst the clouds could be attributed to the incompetence of his subordinates. If the fault wasn't theirs, then it would surely be blamed on any meteorological anomalies that would soon be presented by the looming duster. Hot wires of lightning sizzled through layers of black filth that swelled higher over the horizon with every passing minute.

Partly as a result of the approaching storm, festival attendance had slackened. The most popular events were already over, anyhow. The focus of the activity had boiled down to the farm auction, where the best pieces of machinery were finally up for bid. The majority of attendees were older farmers in straw hats and dusty overalls. The men were gathered in the leeward field, where ranks of tractors, plows, and upwards of a dozen of the self-propelled Baldwin Gleaner combines awaited the auctioneer's attention. While the Baldwin's industry had roared through the twenties, when that prosperous decade with a seemingly endless bounty of wheat came to an end, the terrible drought that had followed plunged more than a few farming companies into bankruptcy. A massive fleet of useless Gleaners, tractors, and a wide assortment of farming implements, were now owned by the bank. With farmer's unions like the Last Man's Club crashing auctions and fixing bids, no one was apt to profit from the widespread loss, but the farmers were making it clear that they weren't going down without a fight. They'd outlast all the companies, every last one of the damned bankers, until there was no one left standing out there in no-man's land but the same settlers around which the entire industry had been built, as they sunk all the way up to the brims of their straw hats in debt to a wasteland that resented them.

A team of volunteer operators stepped up to each of the wayside implements. At the auctioneer's signal, they started every engine at once. Children reared up from their marbles to cover their ears. Black columns of exhaust spewed from the stacks of every tractor and combine on the auction block as a deafening roar ceased all conversation, turned every head, and halted the Rainmaker's pacing. He lowered his bullhorn, shaking his head.

Tufts of blanched fur still shivered on the heaps of barbed wire, a grim memorial to a thousand bygone jackrabbits. Anyone who hadn't attended the festival on opening night would never have guessed that the auction was staged in the exact spot where droves of the varmints had been bludgeoned to death, just two days prior. Their cacophony of dying squeals was but an unpleasant memory burnt into the minds of those who'd witnessed the slaughter. The corral was gone. Their pooled blood and picked bones had been crushed into the dust by the rolling tires of farm machinery, the plodding boots of a few hundred bidders.

The auctioneer shook hands with a banker, smiled stiffly, and raised his bullhorn. As always, it began with a prayer. Pitched to an octave precisely above the combined roar of around fifty engines, the auctioneer's yammering torrent of praise to the Almighty drowned even thunder's deep trundle, as the first drops of moisture began to fall from the sky.

"It's raining," the boy said, smiling at the muddy explosions. Slithering trails of water plied the layer of dust on the windshield. He looked to his Pap with an expression of wonderment. "Ain't we going to get out?"

"What the hell for?"

The boy sighed. He didn't know. It just felt like they should. Everyone else was out there, being involved. As he looked over the activity around Rolla's fairgrounds, anxiety knotted his brow. He wanted to get out of the automobile, to smell the fresh rain, to hear the rapid-firing tongue of the auctioneer, something... Spending a whole day with Pap could be pure torture. He knew better than to ask why they were parked on the outskirts of the festival, and who or what exactly they were waiting for, because he could already anticipate the unsatisfactory response that he'd receive.

"We're waiting on the fire pumper."

Stunned, the boy turned to Pap, eyes blinking, relaxing his grip on the steering wheel. What he'd just heard sounded suspiciously like a straightforward answer. His right knee began to chug, but he put a quick stop to the nervous habit. It was just about killing him to refrain from asking why they were waiting on a fire pumper, but Pap's explanation had come so freely unbidden that the boy was afraid of saying one wrong word that might jeopardize Pap's uncharacteristically forthcoming attitude.

"Rolla's pumper has been kept locked away since Prohibition, when we drove her back from the Weston Distillery with a whole tank full of moonshine—for medical p-purposes, of course." Pap smiled and winked. "We were going to wait until later this evening to go ahead with the plan, but that duster over yonder is apt to block out the sun here in just a matter of minutes, and I guess you know what that means." Pap slapped his hand gently against his knee. "Guess you could say we're ahead of schedule."

The boy ground his molars together, tightening his haunches beneath him. His nose itched, but he didn't dare lift a hand to scratch it. He just wrinkled it, remaining still and silent as a jackrabbit.

"Club dues paid for that fool on the flatbed." Pap pointed a finger in the direction of the Rainmaker. "He was my idea. I reckoned we might need a couple of howitzers for what was sure to come. Turned out it was a whole lot cheaper to rent that clown with his cannons than to go about getting them any other way. Once I'd convinced the mayor to book him, I reckoned they'd go ahead turn it into a big carnival, and some damned banker would surely put up a farm auction. Figured that'd provide us with a nice fleet of bank-owned vehicles to send on into battle, so nobody would have to risk their own. Ye see all them operators sitting up there on them tractors and combines?"

"Yeah." The word "battle" really had the boy's knee chugging away, and this time, he couldn't bring himself to stop it.

"Every one of them is a Club member. So is every bidder in that crowd. That ol' banker's going to shit his britches when the whole auction cuts loose on him, here in just a few more minutes." Pap narrowed his eyes, and sucked at his teeth. "Yes, sir. I'd say it all p-pretty well worked out just the way I'd figured."

The boy's brain felt as though it was frozen. There was really nothing that Pap could say that would've been more interesting than the fact that he was saying it. The boy felt cold, hollowed and ghostly thin—but in a good way, if such a queer feeling were even possible. "Wha—" The boy choked on a knot of questions, and he had to clear his throat.

When Pap turned, his eyes were twinkling with the light of a hundred smiles. He grinned, and gave a satisfied sigh. "Once that fire pumper shows up, we're going to drive her straight out to the Comanche Vent, and dump around a thousand gallons of moonshine right down that vampire hole, light her up, and see what comes a-screechin' out." Pap scratched at his chin whiskers. "That's kind of been the plan for years, but we couldn't bring ourselves to do it, so long as God was still alive. He'd have learned what we was up to, no doubt, and he'd have rustled up a gang and slaughtered us all for sure. He was a vicious sumbitch. Did ye know his whole lineman's contract was nothing a plan for a big ol' v-vampire communication system, running all the way from Liberal out to the Comanche Vent?"

The boy's eyes widened. His knee stopped chugging.

"D-darned right. If he'd been allowed to run them lines, start collaborating over the wires with others of his kind, then there wasn't no way we could've ever stopped him. That would've meant the end of Eden, and surely all of us. That's why I'd never have sold him an easement to get past our section. I was doing my part, but I couldn't do everything myself. He needed killed, but nobody could seem to lay a finger on him—until you came along." Pap winked. "Didn't you wonder how's come I got so shitfaced at the party two nights ago? Every farmer in the county had to come pour me a drink on account of you."

"You mean, everyone knew?" the boy whispered.

"Small town, son." Pap reached over, and patted the boy's skinny knee. "Can't hope to keep a secret that big under wraps for very long in a town of this size. Sure, we all knew what ye done."

The boy's mind flipped through the pages of a mental calendar, scrutinizing the events of every month since Black Sunday. It all seemed so obvious now, in the way that their whole town had suddenly seemed to cut them off. Aside from God—and J.P. and Martha Cobb, of course—there was no traffic past their section in almost two years. It had been so lonely, almost as if they were being shunned. When Mam passed, none but the Cobbs came by to offer condolences, to pay some respects, or even to drop off a danged casserole. He'd never felt so abandoned by the whole living world. Felt like he and Pap were marooned on a desert island clear out in the middle of an ocean of dust.

"Have a look in the seat behind you," Pap said. The fading light danced in his mischievous eyes. White pellets of hail began to rattle upon the roof. Wind moaned out of the west, where the operators perched miserably atop the growling phalanx of machinery tried their best to cover their heads. The wall of darkness muted the pale outline of the noonday sun, as the clanging bell of a fire pumper pealed rhythmically from somewhere off in the distance. "Hurry up. Have ye a look."

The boy rose onto his knees, and turned. There was indeed something hidden beneath a heap of ratty blankets. Something long and tall, with outstretched arms, kind of like the Osage cross atop Mam's hilltop grave. With some hesitation, the boy reached down and peeled back the drab layers of fabric. He sucked in a breath that tickled his hide with what felt like little currents of electricity, and maybe it was, with the duster now upon them. In the vanishing light, the boy admired the golden grain of a varnished Osage crossbow. Hand-carved, and bolstered on the business end with a brass stirrup, riser and gleaming limbs. The weapon was beautiful.

"It's your'n," Pap said. "Carved right from the heart-wood of the same Osage tree as your Mam's ..." Pap nodded, choking just a little on his sentiments. He just smiled, and placed a hand at the base of the boy's neck. "Real p-proud of you, Joe."

The boy lifted the crossbow from behind the seat, and turned to slump back into his seat with the best gift he'd ever been given cradled in his skinny arms. He didn't know what to say. For the first time in his life, he was genuinely speechless.

"Y'know how to use one of these?"

It seemed intuitive enough, but the boy was so stunned that he could only shake his head. He curled his fingers around the taut bowstring, and gave it a weak pull. It didn't budge. He pulled a little harder but the cable beneath his fingers barely dented.

"You ain't going to draw a crossbow like that," Pap said, smiling. "Got to point her downward, slip your boot through that brass stirrup, see, and then use both hands to haul her all the way back until she locks into place. I figured with all of them postholes you've been digging, you might just be wiry enough to get it done."

The boy glanced inquiringly at Pap.

"Go ahead. Stick your foot in there, and give her a real pull."

Lowering the weapon's nose to the floorboards, the boy slid the toe of his boot through the stirrup. He adjusted his position in the driver's seat, took the bowstring in both hands, and pulled until he was standing sideways, quivering like a thistle in the wind. Just a couple of inches short of the brass prong.

"Get mad at it! Pull!"

Lightning sprayed across the sky. Thunder's deafening fusillade shook the Model T to its framework. The boy lifted his rump clear off the seat, gritted his teeth and arched his back, growling into the tempest as he pulled with every ounce of strength that he had. At last, he heard and felt the click of the receiver take the weight of the string from his burning fingers.

"Ye done it, by God!" Pap whooped, and pumped his fist in the air. A clap of thunder unleashed a sheet of rain that wove the outside world into ghostly skeins trailing down the windshield. The boy's brow furrowed. Through the bleary curtain beyond Pap's shoulder, he saw what looked like a dark figure. Rotten palms smacked hard against the glass. The yawning mouth of a vampire sucked up to the window, fangs spurting amber rivulets of pus.

The boy screamed, balling his fist into his mouth. Terrible flashbacks flooded his mind. Hair matted against its face, the monster writhed in the downpour, lolling its gray tongue between the membranes of its fangs, smearing clawed hands up and down the wet glass. It seemed enraptured by the darkness, the seething elements, its proximity to warm-blooded prey.

"Easy, now," Pap said, glancing over his shoulder at the horror mashed against the thin pane. "That's just ol' Grandpappy Cobb, enjoying his first night out in a long while."

The boy slowly withdrew the wadded fist from his lips, gasping as though he'd just resurfaced from a near drowing. He gawped into those coyote eyes, and he could feel the devil himself staring right back from the fires of Hell. "Is he—is he good?"

Pap scowled. "How ye mean, good?"

"Would he hurt us?"

Pap glanced again over his shoulder at the slavering demon. "He'd probably kill the both of us in a heartbeat, if he ever had the chance." Pap grinned. "But I don't reckon these old vampires got any idea how to open the door of a sedan."

In the next instant, the passenger door was ripped wide open. Brimstone stench of the grave came rushing into cab with the roar of warring elements. Thrusting its sodden head through the aperture, the bloodsucker whipped serpentine coils of oily hair over Pap's lap. "Tanker's emptied," it hissed, "fire's lit."

"Well, dang," Pap said, hoisting his eyebrows at the boy. "I guess they was ready to get after it, weren't they?"

"They're coming," it said. The embers of its glare seared a path from Pap to the boy, where they settled to burn hotly on the drawn crossbow. "Best ready ye selves for war." With a flap of its rotten greatcoat, a screech of its claws against metal, the vampire vanished back into the tempest.

"Don't be scratching up my paint, ye sumbitch!" Pap hollered into the torrent. He wrenched the door back closed with a rattling bang, and then swept the water droplets from the greasy chaps of his trousers with a flick of both hands. "Just bought this six months ago, for Christ's sake."

"He didn't kill us."

"What?" Pap looked up, confused, and then broke into a chuckle. "Aw, I was just pulling your leg. He wouldn't hurt us. Loved your Mam to bits and pieces, that old bloodsucker did."

"But I thought they was all coldblooded killers?"

Pap frowned, shaking his head. "Killers, for sure. But when it comes to bloodsuckers, I guess it's kinder like dealing with drunkards. Whoever they was before they got bit, whatever they felt strongest about, that all just kinder gets amplified by the poison. Now, that one, he was always loyal as a dog to his kin, and to anyone else who was friends to his kin. That's why we took ye out to meet him, this morning, so he'd know ye as a friend to J.P. before we took ye into battle."

"Oh..." The boy stared at his Pap until his eyes began to drift. He imagined things. What a strange and different life they might've had, even enjoyed, if Mam's love and devotion to her family had been permitted to be amplified.

Pap narrowed his eyes at the boy. "Regardless of a bloodsucker's temperament, it ain't wise to keep one, so don't get to thinking them dark thoughts. They ain't human, and they'll always need to be fed. Think about that. 'Cause if ye don't feed them, then they'll just start to suck all the life out of everything around them. That's how's come this part of the country came to be such a barren wasteland. All them starving revenants down there in that Comanche Vent had gone and sucked all the life right out of the soil, turned America's heartland into a damned dust bowl."

"You ain't pulling my leg again, are ye?"

Pap shook his head solemnly. "That's the truth of it. They don't even have to bite ye. Living near 'em is bad enough. Only reason the Club allowed J.P. to keep his Great-Grandpappy was because we all knew he could lead us to the Vent. Tomorrow, it'll fall on J.P. to put him down. Monsters like that can't be allowed to exist. Understand?"

The boy blinked, and eventually nodded.

Pap smiled, and patted his knee. "Put her in gear, why don't ye, and follow them Gleaners."

The combines were on the move. The boy dropped the clutch, let his foot slide of the brake, and nosed the throttle level forward. Pap leaned forward to pop the latch at the base of the hinged windshield. He swung the flat pane of glass outward, locking it into an upright position with the prop. He then then reached behind his seat for a quiver of feathered bolts.

"You'd best just drive, until you're strong enough to draw that bowstring a little quicker." Pap took the Osage crossbow by the neck of its stock. He nocked a bolt to the drawn string, and snapped it down against the brass riser. "If we get a chance, I'll let you take a shot."

The boy trailed the growling phalanx of Gleaner combines out into the field, where they assumed a V-shaped formation that was not unlike the human funnel employed in the jackrabbit drive. Once the rolling armada was in place, every driver engaged his header. Bladed cylinders began to spin like enormous meat grinders. Through sheets of muddy rain, the boy could discern the forms of several men perched atop each combine. He could account for their numbers by the glow of lanterns and blowtorches, as the line rumbled directly for the storm's black heart, where the glow of a distant bonfire raged on the dark horizon.

"I thought ye didn't want to risk our any of our own vehicles?" the boy said, knowing that it was a little late to do anything about the fact that they were rolling into battle in Pap's beloved Model T.

"You just drive careful."

The boy wiped the filth from his eyes, but to little avail. Mud sprayed through the open windshield, painting their faces with elemental pigments matched only by the blackness of the sky. Ricocheted hailstones bounced off the dash to clatter crazily around the Model T's metal interior. If this wasn't the road to Hell, then he couldn't imagine any worse place to which such a direction could lead. The groan of gathering winds muted the roar of the farmers' armada. The skies pulsed with electricity, until a white arm of lightning shot straight down from the clouds to crush a Gleaner in a fist of orange fire.

"Holy smokes! Did you see that, Pap?"

Pap didn't reply. He was screeding mud from one eye with a knuckle as the militia parted to thunder past the wayward machine. Its crew of flaming farmers pitched from the fenders to roll in the mud. The new gap in the line closed. The formation retightened, and kept pushing full-throttle ahead.

Ahead, the great bonfire toward which they bore appeared to spread like flowing lava across the hellscape. The boy squinted his eyes. The lake of fire seemed to be broken in places, as if it were not a solid wall of flames at all, but rather, a whole field of smaller fires rushing toward them.

"Pap?"

"Fall back!" Pap shouted. "Let them Gleaners take the brunt of it. You and I can pick off any that make it through the line."

The boy throttled down until the Model T fell between the ranks of a second force that he hadn't even realized was tailing them. This wave was comprised of tractors. Two were towing the howitzers. The rest were hitched to plows that disked up great wakes of muck from beneath their racks of gleaming blades. The boy's eyes widened in the side mirror. Behind the tractors was an army of foot soldiers. Every bidder from the auction was armed with a melee weapon seasoned two days prior with the blood of a thousand jackrabbits. Chains, wrenches and pitchforks glimmered by the light of a hundred torches.

At once, he could hear them. Piercing the darkness with a promise for bloodshed came a discordant scream more terrible than the cry of a billion jackrabbits. The sound was not one that could've possibly been produced by the militia of farmers. It was the sound of something worse. It was them.

Donning uniform coats of moonshine flames, the burning army of bloodsuckers unleashed its pandemoniac war cry as Hell's foot soldiers charged headlong into the line of Baldwin Gleaners. Molten forms slammed into the whirling blades, where they were rent apart like wads of burning paper. Bodies exploded in fiery chuffs as they were dragged shrieking into the terrible machines, pulverized into burning hash that fountained from the combines' auger spouts. Dramatic plumes of brimstone sparks joined the elemental fervor of howling wind, soil and rain, broadcasted like fertilizer over the same fields under which they'd crept for untold ages.

By the primal rage that fueled their screams, the boy guessed these warriors to be the ancient ones, those nameless denizens of bygone windows of time long before this wasteland was familiar with cart or horse. Unable to fathom the destructive power of a modern armada that was designed to devour all life in its path, the aboriginals charged headlong into oblivion. However, when the Great War howitzers thundered in concert, spewing dragon fire as burning payloads of cordite blasted gaps through the wall of screaming fire, the enemy ranks suddenly wheeled. Just like a herd of jackrabbits before the drivers, they attempted to flee the encroaching force in a hopeless retreat.

Those that stumbled were trampled underfoot in the chaos, or passed unscathed beneath the whirling razor headers. These few had time enough to rise smoldering and bewildered from the mud before the second wave of tractors roared over them. The boy watched their bodies tumble beneath the tills, neatly segmenting between the blades into uniformly burning slices.

"Heads up," Pap said, as a cagey pair dodged the second wave. They charged straight for the Model T. Pap leveled the crossbow over the dashboard, squeezed the trigger, and sent a cedar bolt screaming through the first bloodsucker's hijacked brain. As the warrior toppled, Pap's boot was already in the stirrup, heaving to the bowstring. The second monster was coming fast. Before Pap could nock a bolt, the burning creature had smashed into the grill, and began to claw its way upon the automobile's hood.

"Don't scratch up the paint!"

"Shoot him, Pap! Shoot him!"

Pap fumbled a cedar shaft from the quiver as the thing dragged its bubbling carcass over the metal, looking for all the earth like another demon of the boy's nightmares, hissing like a prairie rattlesnake as venom whipped from its gaping maw. Even through its mask of flame, sloughing

150

skin, the tattooed glyphs of some ancient sect still streaked its cheeks. The boy shouted as its hand struck out, snatching the steering wheel in a skeletal grip. Though it couldn't have known the purpose of the device, it wrenched the wheel starboard in its fervor to pull itself inward, whipping the automobile into a tractor's flank. The force of the collision was tremendous. With a cascade of glass, a second blow was dealt by the massive trailer of discs, and the Model T was rolled onto its side.

The boy slowly regained his rattled bearings as the line of tractors growled away. Whooping foot soldiers stampeded through the mud on either side. They streamed around the incapacitated vehicle until their cries of battle had left the boy and his Pap behind. A volley of shrieks and blunt impacts suggested that the infantry had engaged the remnants of the crushed enemy force. The boy could only listen to the commotion. He couldn't move. A great weight pressed down upon him, pinning him to the driver's side door. It wasn't until he heard the rhythmic tapping, and realized that the sound was falling droplets of blood, that he noticed the weight upon him was his Pap. A wide gash yawned across the man's forehead. He wasn't moving.

"Pap?" The boy grabbed his shoulder. He gave him a good shaking, but Pap's battered head just jostled around on his leathery neck. The stark implications of what might be a new life without his Pap snapped through the boy's mind. It wasn't running the business that worried him, nor was it the details of managing the homestead. The only thing doomed to forever remain in a state of disrepair if Pap was snatched out of his life would be the gaping hole in his heart left behind by the missing guy who was, and always had been, his best friend.

"Pap!"

No response. Only the steady spatter of falling droplets, and the sluice of drizzling fluid outside the automobile. The boy covered his nose with the back of his wrist, choking on heady fumes of gasoline. He growled as he strained to escape the smothering bulk of Pap's body. When the weight finally shifted, there came a woody clatter, like a mess of falling twigs. Took the boy a second to realize that the damned quiver was pinned between them. Bolts had spilled from the leather cylinder down into every recess of the canted automobile, providing an added hazard of jutting points at every turn. The boy crooked the bend of his arm around his Pap's neck, gripped the wheel, and began the task of dragging his unconscious father out through the open windshield.

Gasoline slopped from the slain Model T in pinkish spurts the color of watery blood. The boy coughed and squinted his burning eyes in the astringent cloud that somehow hung over them despite the howling gale, the curtains of harried dust. Standing up to his ankles in a lake of fuel, he turned his head in the direction of whoops and cheering. The battle had evidently been won. Silhouettes of dancing farmers hoisted crossbows in the air, resembling an army of victorious knights celebrating some glorious crusade. Beyond the littered battlefield gleamed a pale edge to the western sky, like a light at the end of a dark tunnel. It was passing over. On the black duster's trailing edge gleamed the promise of the midday sun.

A burning hand, and then the smoldering form appeared, leering around the tipped automobile. The boy froze in the glare of its yellow eyes, as they fixed on him. Its yawning mouth emitted the hiss of steam escaping Hell's gates. The melted folds of tattooed flesh stretched into the most terrible grin, as twin membranes pulled taut around translucent fishhooks. The monster seemed to recognize that its war was lost, but there remained a chance to take the life of one, last child. Ropes of viscous venom oozed from its fangs, to be licked away with one sweep of the creature's gray tongue. Planting one clawed hand mechanically before the other, it dragged its shattered and burning hindquarters through the mud. Pale splinters of protruding bone tilled rows through the muck.

The boy seized his Pap around the breadbasket and pulled with all his might, slipping in the widening pool of gasoline that mirrored the infernal image of that horror cast upon it. As his Pap finally tumbled through the windshield, and down into the bath of fuel, a wavering groan escaped his throat. He was still alive.

An indignant hiss from the monster's gaping throat seemed a resentful sentiment against the slightest hope for life. Flames crackling down its spine, the revolting husk hitched its way through the black slime, threads of venom whipping from the cusp of its chin. When its steaming claws plunged into the gasoline, it hesitated. Lowering its drooling chin, the thing gawped down into the swirling lake of fuel with an expression of profound ignorance.

Releasing his embrace around his Pap, the boy lunged instead for the crossbow propped against the steering column. Not one more inch. The boy swung the weapon around as the vampire raised its head with a mindless smile.

"Tell God howdy for me, if ye wouldn't mind," the boy said, curling his finger around the trigger, releasing the empty bowstring with a hollow snap.

Although the ancient creature had no comprehension of automobiles, Gleaners, or of fuel's combustibility, it did seem to understand the turn of tables presented by an enemy's dry-fired bow. The monster threw back its charred head to emit sputtering laughter rough as a sawyer's blade through dry wood. Plunging its other hand into the fuel, its burning glare of hate fell onto Pap, as every sinew in its body tightened for what was to be its final lunge.

The peal of the clanging bell softened its countenance, melting predatory resolve into the confounded visage of prey. That was to be the last face worn by the ancient bloodsucker, as the tires of Rolla's fire pumper crushed its tattooed skull with a wet pop. Instantly, hundreds of false years swept over its cheating body, withering flesh to curled ribbons, bones into dust, until only a smoldering heap remained.

Pap groaned, and lolled his head. The boy fell to his rump in the pool of gasoline with a splash. Squinting into the light of the emerging sun, he found enough strength left in him to raise a hand in thanks to the grinning face of J.P., who was peering down from behind the pumper's wheel. Seated stiffly beside him in the passenger seat was the corpse of his Great-Grandpappy.

"What the hell did ye do to my Model T?" Pap said, tilting his bloodied head toward the wrecked automobile.

In the distance, old farmers were slapping backs, picking weird souvenirs off the battlefield. Jugs of moonshine had appeared out of nowhere, as they always seemed to do, and were already making their way through the crowd, lip to lip, and hand to hand. At last, the nightmare was over.

The attack on the Comanche Vent had been so perfectly coordinated. A hideout for ancient evil that had existed unmolested for so many millennia had been raided, pillaged, and its warriors blown to Kingdom Come. All of that thanks to Pap, the same man whom the boy had sorely mistaken for an old fool on so many occasions. One swing, and he'd knocked one clean out of the park.

"We done it, Pap. You did. It's over."

Pap grumbled, looking away from the ruin of his beloved Model T, blinking his eyes. He dabbed at the wound on his forehead, and inspected the blood on his fingertips. "Just bought that sumbitch six months ago."

The glimmering battlefield was hammered to the horizon in every direction with pocks of heavenly water. The sun hung brightly in the bluebird sky. The smell of soil, rich and loamy, hung in the moistened air. In the distance, the Rainmaker was already trumpeting into his bullhorn, no doubt seizing the moment to plunder his share of the credit for all that had just transpired. Folks all around were laughing and carrying on. Corn whiskey was flowing. It was going to be a beautiful day.

Everyone jumped at the thunderous concussion of an army howitzer. Heads turned to the west, where a crackling bloom of burning minerals flowered on high. Another explosion. A white strobe flashed and sizzled, dribbling glittering streamers of phosphorus all the way back down to the earth. The fireworks evoked a great cheer from the Last Man's Club, and a honk of disdain from the Rainmaker, at the evident waste of his precious commodities.

"We paid for it, ye sumbitch," Pap grumbled, as J.P. helped lift him to his feet, "and we can blow it all up if we want to."

"Here we go now," J.P. said, throwing Pap's arm over his shoulders, leading him toward the fire pumper.

The boy's skin burned from the gasoline. His clothing reeked. He didn't imagine that any amount of soap and scrubbing would take the stink of the petrol off him. Might have to resort to a bath in tomato juice, just as if he'd been sprayed by a skunk.

"God dang, do we have to take him with us?" Pap exclaimed, at the sight of the vampire corpse in the passenger seat.

"Now, Lionel, wouldn't be right if we didn't give him a Christian burial," J.P. replied. "We couldn't have done any this today, if it weren't for my Great-Grandpappy."

"Well, how's about moving him in back? He kinder stinks."

Bemused by the banter of the two older men, the boy shouldered his crossbow, and strode out past the pumper for a last look at the battlefield. Already, it was beginning to evolve from a place of slaughter to something resembling a big party. The boy nodded his head. He knew for sure that his Pap had done the right thing. That bright sunshine on his face was his Mam, smiling down on him like the angel she'd always been. Thanks to Pap, he'd never have to remember her any other way.

"I love ye, Mam," he whispered, blinking back a couple of sudden tears, "and I'll always miss ye." The boy didn't guess that he'd ever feel the urge to pull a swig of corn whiskey again, but today just might be an exception. He wiped the back of his hands across his eyes, sniffed, and when his vision cleared, he had to rub them a second time in an effort to erase the sight seared upon them.

Erupting from their burning underworld as a solid plume of blackness charred against the sky, they billowed up like volcanic ash from the pits of Hell. Something yet remained unsettled. Something stirred, down below, and it wasn't a bloodsucker. As much as those things resembled bats, the boy knew better. They were a part of it. All of them. Collective souls of a revenant spirit that leeched all life within its reach. There was a bat for every slaughtered buffalo, a bat for every tilled blade of bluestem, a bat for every fallen Indian, and somewhere up there amongst that swarm, there was probably even a bat for his Mam. The spirit had found her in her final moments, fastened itself upon her body and soul, and the boy knew with dread certainty that she would never find peace, none of them would, until the entity that had consumed them was finally put to rest. It didn't appear that he'd need to go far to hunt it down, or even to crawl down into the pit where it festered.

It was coming to him.

Rumbling of godlike resonance shook the earth beneath his feet. No fireworks display followed this one. No howitzer had been fired. A tremendous upheaval toppled men all around, as if great cogs in the engines of the earth itself had lurched quite suddenly into motion. The battlefield trembled, rippling with concentric waves as though solid ground had become the surface of some vast pond. Something heaved upward, tipping both howitzers onto their sides, and an ocean of water beneath the dry land oozed to the surface. Gleaners and tractors began to sink, as starved land drew down all things set upon it. A collective cry of despondence arose from the cowering masses. Boots bogged in the slurry of soil and water. Bravado devolved to terror, as no-man's land sucked farmers down to the bibs of their overalls.

The boy took a few steps backward. A quarter-mile behind the lines of the battlefield, it was not so treacherous. Water squished beneath his boots, and it pooled around the pumper, but the vehicle remained afloat. They were castaways lost in the heart of an inland sea, one haunted by a Kraken that threatened to erase all evidence of the blow that humankind had just dealt it.

With the roar of ten tornadoes, cloaked in the filth of a dozen black dusters, the leviathan breached through a tear in the wasteland to unfurl wings so vast they eclipsed the sun. Burning eyes like portals to Hell bulged from a featureless face with only a gash for a ragged mouth. Unleashing an elephantine bellow, the horror knuckled across the battlefield, soil cascading from its humped back, as it trundled toward the island of awestruck castaways. It diverted its charge to fold occasionally at its midsection, slamming its saw-toothed maw over the heads of bogged farmers like a galactic Gleaner of all earthly life. Here was the harvester of harvesters, the header of all headers, throttling down rows of a human crop that was ready to reap.

The boy lowered his crossbow from his shoulder. He slipped his boot through the brass stirrup, and took the string in both hands. This probably wasn't the first time in its long life that the great bat had seen fit to quit its lair, to answer to a human challenger. The ancient tribes had almost certainly encountered it. The mound builders. The grave diggers. The tattooed nomads whose warier successors thought to raise their dead on high scaffolds to place them out of reach whatever dwelt beneath this soured land. The boy heaved to the cable in the Thunderbird's shadow, pulling until he heard the click of the brass receiver, and the string's weight was taken from his hands.

"It was you, all along, wasn't it?" the boy said, narrowing his eyes at the collector of souls, fountainhead of vampires, the great leech of the Ogallala Aquifer that had nearly suckled the dust bowl dry. Parasite, harvester, destroyer and living god, it glowered down upon the boy, reeking with its otherworldly brimstone stink. "What the hell are you, anyhow?"

The Thunderbird reared, spreading the black membranes of its dragon wings. Its bellow resonated over the wastelands, as it proclaimed some entitlement as apex predator of this world, as king of this barren sanctum of its earthly domain. When its lungs were finally depleted, the behemoth folded at the midsection, knuckling down over the boy with its serrated jaws sprung wide to receive him.

The boy reached into his boot. He withdrew the same weapon that he'd kept holstered there every day since Black Sunday, the same stake that had pierced the black heart of

God. Forged by hellfire and lightning, slickened with blood and rendered fat of a slain demon, his trusty Comanche had seen better days, for sure. The boy nocked the arrow to his bowstring, and he snapped the shaft down tightly against the riser. He relished the slickness of varnished Osage in his grip, as he swung the crossbow upward to put a bead right between those fiery eyes.

What was it about wood? There was just something timeless about the smell and feel of polished heartwood, the mesmerizing current of oceanic swirls in wooden grain, that all seemed to harken back to the ancient craft of shaping wood into perfect weapons admired by boys being shaped into dragon slayers.

As he curled his finger around the brass trigger, he reckoned the only thing missing on this nearly perfect weapon was just a little bit of personalized character. The boy squinted his shooting eye, and grinned. All it needed was a notch.

< END >